Mel was dying by inches and wasn't having fun. Her brother was dead, her niece was trying to take care of things, and her brother's parrot was cursing a blue streak.

Leaving Earth for a reset sounded simple, but she was too large for the canisters and had to be launched across space in a separate ship, still growing. She goes through three species who want her genetics, but the first two drop out, and finally, she wakes up on a space station with gravity so strong she can barely stand up.

Mel meets the station, watches her parrot enjoy the heavy-gravity flight and tries to get a handle on what happens next when no one will tell her what is going on.

She takes a new friend home, heads back to her shuttle, and accidentally sparks an incident that puts a price on her head but helps her gain perspective. Mel has a place in the stars, and she is finding it.

PIRATE BY PARROT
TERRAN RESET, BOOK 9

BY

VIOLA GRACE

CHAPTER ONE

Mel looked to her left as she moved slowly into the gazebo, where her guest was already seated. "Why don't you just die already?"

Marco squawked, *"Why don't you just die already?"*

Mel grinned. "I am trying; I am trying." She coughed as she laughed. Bloody flecks were caught in a tissue and stuffed into her pocket with the others.

"I would shake your hand, but mine is gross. So, what can I do for you?"

"Do you remember signing up for the Volunteer Project a few decades ago?"

Mel nodded and coughed into a fresh tissue. She wheezed. "Yeah. That ship sailed with a thud."

"What would you say if I offered you another chance? We

have need of people like you for specific assignments."

"I am not going to last long enough to get out of the atmosphere, let alone into deep space." She pressed her teeth together as she chuckled, and Marco chortled.

"I am sorry for not introducing myself. I am Minerva-Gaia. I am currently running the Volunteer Program. Well, we are referring to it as the Terran Reset Program for now. We need you for a very specific assignment on a very specific world."

She sipped at the water glass that her niece had brought out. "You like the word specific."

Minerva grinned and rubbed the back of her neck. "We need you. Your genetic makeup will be ideal for being remade into a young, healthy giantess."

Mel paused. "What the actual fuck? I am already six foot two with emphysema and lung cancer."

"Smoking?"

"Waitressing. I had to wade through the smoke day after day with no reprieve. They could have a cigarette and leave, but I was stuck as dozens of smokers lit up at the same time."

Minerva nodded. "I understand, but your life expectancy has pushed you to the front of the line for urgency, so we contacted your match, and they are willing to take possession of you as soon as possible.

"Wait. Match? Are you running a mail-order bride service?" She laughed, and Marco chuckled along.

"Yes, and no. We are using tech that can rebuild you and reset your biological clock in an effort to build ties with worlds we would otherwise have no chance with. One lady is fireproof; another has strength that would be the envy of any comic book hero."

"And I am to be a giant if I agree?"

"Your genes predispose you to height; we just have to build up the mass and get you ready for a new gravity."

"More gravity?"

"Less."

"Oh, so... less gravity, more height? Interesting."

Minerva smiled and said, "As I was saying, your illness would be eradicated and your lungs made whole again. You would be younger, taller, and given all the energy and dexterity of youth. Getting used to your new dimensions would be accounted for, and your new wardrobe would fit your new body. A financial arrangement would be set up so that at no time will you feel obligated to your new intimate situation, but you would be required to pick a partner from your new world. The idea is to check to see if altered Terran genetics are strong enough to carry on a new line."

"Wow. Just putting it out there. So, why me?"

"Why me? Why me? Whiney beggar."

Mel looked at the bird. "What do you know? As soon as I am gone, they are going to put your patchy ass to sleep."

He squawked and flapped at her. *"Mouthy bitch!"*

She grinned, and Minerva stared. "That's your bird?"

"It was my brother's. He's passed, and his kids don't want poor Marco." She smiled and sighed. "He used to ride on my shoulder, but since the coughing has kicked up, it freaks him out."

Minerva looked thoughtful. "What if you could take your bird?"

Mel stared. "What?"

"You could take him with you. He would be reworked and given a new lease on life so that you wouldn't be out there alone."

Mel looked at her splotchy bird and then at the woman in the gracefully designed armoured suit with a gauzy long vest. "What kind of clothing would I end up with?"

"The Cekkaro dress like this." A projection of a male with a silky tunic, leather pants, and a sturdy build was suddenly in the middle of the gazebo.

"What about the ladies?"

"They don't have them. They went to a cloned population a few hundred years ago and are now suffering from clone collapse."

"Oh, the copy factor."

Minerva nodded. "Yeah. So, you would be welcome to design your own wardrobe or just dress like the dudes."

The reference made Mel laugh, and then she coughed.

"Why don't you use a mask and tank?"

"Why prolong things? I am a huge fan of getting things over with, and I have already lived far longer than my doctor guessed at."

Minerva nodded. "Fair enough."

"If I say yes, when can I go?"

"Get your things in legal order so that all heirs are accounted for, and I will pick you up in hours."

"Done. Already done. You can't live like this and not take care of things. My niece gets it all."

"Excellent. Well then, I will just offer you this contract. It outlines what you are volunteering for and what we will provide you with, including security."

She took it and signed it.

Minerva gasped. "Don't you want to read it?"

"Nope. Die here, or die there. I am up for a change of

scenery as long as I can bring Marco along."

"A second contract involving Marco is being prepared, and my assistant will be in with it momentarily. The addenda will be connected to your contract."

"You have minions?"

Minerva laughed. "Yes. My husband makes sure that someone has my back at all times."

"Is he as snappy a dresser as you are?"

Minerva chuckled. "More so. He's running a few of the other Reset ladies into space. You are going to be our test with a new contractor."

Mel chuckled. "Sounds like fun. Do they get a bonus if I am delivered?"

"They do, but all healing and alterations are going to happen on the Lunar Base. We don't trust them with the tech we are using or the extremely rare genetic samples we are pairing." She smiled. "You will be spending a lot of time with my daughter. Alyla."

Mel smiled. "You have a daughter?"

"Yes. She's going to be an only child in all likelihood. Imbolt is a bit much on the genetic scale and highly radioactive at close range."

"At least he's warm." Mel chuckled.

There was a squawk. *"Hot as fuck!"*

Minerva stared at the bird. "He has quite the grasp of language."

"My brother ran a strip club. It was a competition to get nasty phrases to stick. I don't even hear them anymore." She smiled and then coughed wildly and slowly sucked air in as blood bubbled out. "Your timing is incredible."

Mel looked at the other woman as her vision straightened, and things came back into focus. The grey was fading more slowly with every massive seizure. Not really a good sign.

"Get off your knees, bitch!"

She flipped her bird off and leaned back in her chair. The delicate fan-back framed her, and she could see her skin was flushed and grey at the same time. She wondered what season her colour palette currently was.

She leaned back in the chair and got her breathing under control.

Minerva looked at her. "May I help?"

"What are you thinking?"

"Well, Gaia would like you able to survive the trip to space, so I need to put in a patch of some sort."

"Will it hurt?"

"You don't like pain?"

"Nope. But I can deal. I just like some warning so I can plan my epithets." She wheezed.

Minerva smiled and got up, pressing her hand to Mel's chest, lining it up with the bronchial pathways and filling her lungs with a soothing warmth.

Mel breathed in slowly, and a tear trickled from her eye. "Thanks for that. I didn't think I was going to make it to the shuttle."

Minerva stroked her hair. "You have done a lot in your life. Server, ambulance driver, combat medic, and back to server. You have lived a life and touched many others."

"I got around." Mel leaned back with her eyes closed and just breathed. She heard motion by the door and opened her tired eyes.

A man in an astonishingly fitted business suit came toward them with another tablet. He frowned when he saw her, but it was a worried look. She gave him a thumbs-up. "So, am I signing for me or the parrot?"

He smiled. "For yourself. The parrot will sign first."

Minerva took the tablet and went to speak to Marco. The woman's eyes were glowing, and Marko bobbed his head in excitement. The tablet was held up to line up with the bird's eye, and there was a bright scan. The claw came out next and pressed into the tablet.

Minerva, with glowing eyes, smiled as Marko flapped excitedly.

She turned toward Mel and said, "My little feathered child is excited. She dreams of the stars."

Mel sat up. "She?"

"Yes. She. She likes you very much and wants to continue as your companion, so hers was a companion agreement for emotional assistance."

"Wow. Marko, I guess you need a name change."

Minerva turned back and then smiled. "She likes Marko. It has been her name all her life. If you want to change it, just add a syllable."

"Markona is as far as I will take it, Marko. Promise."

The bird bobbed excitedly and flapped as she screamed.

Minerva nodded. "Now, this is a companion agreement for you so that she is registered to you and you alone until either of you pass on. She is being adapted to all environments and will even be able to fly in space if necessary. She will be, in your parlance, the sturdiest fucking bird in history."

Mel started laughing and held her hand up. Marko glided toward her and climbed up to her shoulder. They nuzzled together, and Marko began to groom her hair.

Minerva smiled. "There are creatures that have been designed for this kind of a response, and I think this is what they are shooting for. Calm caring."

"Will the alterations hurt Marko?"

"No. We are using the same tech we are using on you. Marko will grow slowly and with balance so that flight is never in danger."

"Oh, good." She took the tablet and read it. It was basically swearing that Marko would be with her until death. "Yeah, we always knew that."

She signed it, pressed her thumb, and stared at the optic scanner. She handed it back to Minerva and handed both tablets to her assistant. "Link and upload them to the archive. I will help Mel and Marko to the car."

He blinked. "You are going with us?"

"I am. She requires immediate assistance without notice. I am equipped for it, and I want to hug my daughter."

"That is why you wore your suit." He chuckled.

"Correct." She held out her hand to Mel. "Come on, Melora, Marko, your future awaits."

Mel put her hand in the slim woman's and accepted the help. She called her lawyer and told him to transfer all of her assets to Pria. She got one hug from her niece and spoke quickly to her, explaining what was happening. All assets were hers to keep or dispose of, and Mel was taking Marko to space. It sounded crazy, but it was all summed up.

Mel looked at Alyla over the breathing apparatus they had fitted to her until her alterations started kicking in. They normally did that kind of thing in transit, but she was a special case, and so was Marko.

It had been a month in the tank to reset her body, and now she was working through the genetic fusion.

She smiled. "Hey, Alyla. How are things going?"

"Well, I have come to announce that your lungs are good, and you are ready to start walking around in the cargo hold."

"The hold?"

"You have outgrown the med bay." Alyla grinned. "Mom will be impressed."

"Do I need the mask?"

"Can you breathe comfortably without it?"

"Yeah."

"Take it off." Alyla grinned. "We have a transport tank that will work on your density. You are really coming along. Hell, you are taller than my dad."

Mel looked at Marko's perch, and her buddy was preening

her new silvery feathers. She had quadrupled in size, and that was the point where Mel figured out that it was in her future, too.

She slowly removed the mask and hung it up. She could breathe just fine, but she snored. The mask helped.

She slowly stood up and now towered over Alyla. "Well, my admiration for your mother just increased."

"Why?"

"Because I have seen pictures of her with your father, and I can tell you that I feel terrifying."

Marko flew to her shoulder and settled. The loose trousers and tunic flowed around her as they walked to the cargo area that had been blocked off and turned into an apartment.

"Aw, this is so sweet!"

Alyla grinned. "It is the least we could do. I know that you felt every ache and pain as you grew."

"Pain lets you know you are still alive. I don't like it, but at least I can move on my own now." She chuckled. "Your mom is on my holiday card list."

Marko chirped for permission and took off in the enormous and vaulted space.

"We are also working on a suit that will compete with your growth."

"Split it into trousers and a top, put stretch zones along the seams, and make the top into a butt-covering tunic so it can rise up."

"Any decoration?"

"A fancy sash to make it feel fun. I wear a fucking parrot, after all."

Alyla chuckled. "I saw the sketches you have been making. They are hilarious."

"Woo fucking hoo! Out of my way, jerkass!" Marko was doing barrel rolls, her silver feathers gleaming.

"Ah, I can fall asleep to that." She chuckled and enjoyed not wheezing and hacking afterward.

"We are trying to ship you out and are building a canister for the final development and density issues. You won't get too much taller, but your final density is going to require reinforcing your bones and strengthening muscle attachments."

"Really? I thought I was going to a lighter gravity species." She frowned.

Alyla blinked. "Mom said she was going to tell you. They fell through, so your genetics were offered to Skevarik. They jumped at the chance, so to speak, and you are now destined for the Nyal Imperium."

"Oh, right. I remember something of my final form not being certain for one species. Uh, so, I need different language lessons."

Alyla nodded. "This is why I wanted to get you situated here and started with a light exercise regimen. We don't have a trainer your size, but we will make do."

Mel chuckled. "I was never good at yoga, but I was great at basic training."

"Interesting, and we will take that under advisement. First, we need to get you some clothing and shoes. The shoes are the rough part."

"Yup. I can imagine. Sandals will be a good start. Everything should be wrap and tie capable until I finish growing."

"Yes, ma'am. Are you good here?"

"Yup. You said, Skevarik?"

"Yes. They are giant heavy-worlders."

"Oh. Great. I thought that didn't happen."

"There are exceptions to everything, and that includes genetic design." Alyla smiled. "I am one, and you are one, so why not others?"

"See you for checkers?"

"Three hours and counting. I just have to send some things

off and make a few calls, but hopefully, I will come bearing snacks and a change of clothing for you."

"Cool. Where is the dispensing unit?"

"Next to the large display. How is your dexterity?"

"Better since I filed my fingernails." She looked at her nails.

"We need a mani-pedi night."

"I don't know if you have enough polish."

Alyla grinned. "We have industrial acrylic. I can make it whatever colour I want. See you in a few hours."

Mel looked around at her long bed, a stand for Marko, along with food, water, and treats, and a couch. It was a step up from medical, and she looked at the open space around the temporary wall and started doing push-ups and jumping jacks to start getting used to more powerful limbs.

She had been prepared to go all light and airy, but now, she was going to be a thudding monster. She could deal with that.

Marko flew around and shrieked curses until she settled on the wall to watch Mel working out.

* * * *

Alyla looked at the monitor showing Mel's activities, and she was growing by leaps and bounds. Her body was under her control, and she wasn't suffering from the altitude. It was glorious. She had gotten genes from one of the last Skevarik queens. There were other females, but they weren't what Alyla was looking at. Mel was a warrior in every move, and her body wanted to continue its progress.

CHAPTER TWO

Mel looked at her friend from the confines of the tank. "You are sure about this?"

"Yup. Your canister is set for you. You are ready to head off to the supply station, and from there, you will be picked up by the Skevarik. You are going to be asleep the whole time, and Marko is watching over you. She has a bunch of alerts that she can trigger if you go off course or something goes wrong."

"Okay. It is a cuckoo and canary on Earth to alert and warn of disaster, but I will take a giant parrot in a spaceship."

"The ship we are sending you in is a heavily armed and armoured drone. It is programmed to get you to that station safely, and from there, you can come out, and you need to call me immediately. I worry."

"Yes, miss. Send flowers to your mother tomorrow. It's Mother's Day, and it's important that she feel appreciated."

Alyla stood with the medical team. "Got it. Ready to travel?"

"How long will I be under?"

"Four months. This pod is heavily defended and fully supplied for years. It won't take years. If we don't hear from you in five months, we are going to have every seer and tracker that we have in search of you. You will need to remain on heavy-grav worlds, or you will have side effects. The density programming starts the moment you leave here."

Mel put one hand up, and Alyla clasped it, blinking as they smiled. "Right. Operation mail-order giant commences as soon as I am out, with the expansion pack of a cussing cyber parrot standing by."

Alyla put her hand down and tucked Mel's hand back into the capsule. The team went to work, and everything went black.

* * * *

Marko watched the stars go past. It was wonderful. So many places to fly, and her favourite person to be her companion. It had been kind of Gaia to provide a companion for the strangeness of space, but Melora was a good companion. She was strong, she was funny, and she encouraged vocalizations of any kind.

Marko chuckled and looked through the tiny viewing window in the long tube that held Mel. Mel was changing colour. She was going from her plucked skin colour to a beautiful and vibrant blue with red hands. She was finally looking like she was supposed to be. Her hair was vibrant green in keeping with the contract that Gaia had arranged.

Marko's feathers had turned glossy silver, but Mel now wore the colours. It was right that they didn't die. She was going to look splendid. Marko looked to the front of the empty vessel. She wondered what colour Mel's mate would be.

* * * *

Mel felt the capsule blow open and breathed in air that did not smell like Lunar Base. It wasn't bad, just different.

"Get up, bitch!" Marko was at the edge of the opening and moving from side to side rapidly.

Mel struggled up, and she looked at her limbs in

comparison to the opening. She was six inches taller at least, and she felt weighed down.

"Call me!"

She looked around. The shuttle was gone, and the pod was all that was left.

The ceilings of the station she was on were a comfortable twenty feet, and a light was cascading further into the hallways, letting Marko lead the way. The silvery wings were definitely developed, and Mel staggered after her, bracing herself on the wall as she followed her buddy.

The lights in the station kept directing her, and she moved slowly until a com unit was found under the grip of Marko's claws. Marko was squawking, and Mel staggered to the terminal and put in the code for the lunar station.

She braced herself against the wall, and to her amusement, a chair whirred in. Surprisingly, it was scaled for her.

"Thank you."

"You are welcome," a deep male voice reverberated in the chamber.

She jumped, but Marko remained calm, so she waited for the call to go through.

Alyla's face flared into the screen. *"Mel! Where are you?"*

"Uh. No clue. Trace the call."

The voice came out again. "Vendori Station. The pod was jettisoned here six weeks ago."

Alyla stared. *"Jettisoned?"*

"The vessel the pod was on was under attack. Once the pod was safe, the vessel drew fire and proceeded with all speed."

Alyla paused. *"Is that the station talking?"*

Mel shrugged. "I dunno. I have been awake less than an hour."

"Yes, miss, it is the station. The Vendori have been notified of her arrival, but as she is contained, they are not in a hurry to make their way here."

Mel sat back and said, "Am I even needed for this?"

Alyla sighed. *"The Skevarik are claiming that we are not upholding the contract."*

The station answered that. "The Skevarik were the ones attacking the pod."

Alyla blinked. *"Do you have video?"*

"Yes, and communications recordings. They did not see the vessel drop the pod."

Alyla paused. *"Why did the ship drop the pod?"*

"Marko asked them to."

Mel looked at her bird. "Did you do that, you clever lady?"

Marko hopped onto her shoulder and started grooming

her hair. Mel noticed quickly that her hair was bright green, her hands were dark red, and a glance into her suit said her body was dark blue. She looked at Marko, and the silver bird kept preening her hair. She knew those colours.

The ship stated, "Recordings have been sent."

Alyla nodded. "*Received. Thank you. This is not going to be a quiet issue.*"

"Did we ever get clothing for me?"

"*How tall are you?*"

"The subject is two point six metres tall," the station stated. "Clothing is being fabricated in the available materials based on style options offered by Marko. Her systems are very easy to speak with."

Marko fluffed her feathers.

Mel chuckled and made affection sounds that made Marko lean in, and they touched heads.

Alyla smiled. "*Well, I am glad that you aren't there alone. Vendori Station, do you have food?*"

"Yes, miss."

"*Okay. Good. Will you let me access this terminal again for an inbound call?*"

"Of course, miss."

Alyla looked at Mel. "*Mel, we are going to sort this out.*"

"Good, because it is hard to move this body around. I am going to have to work out hard."

Alyla smiled. *"You have never shied away from hard work. Get hopping."*

Mel made a face, and Marko pitched in, *"Fuck off, bitch!"*

"What the bird said."

Alyla laughed and said, *"I will be in touch in a few days. I am getting to the bottom of this."* She ended on a grim note, *"I am calling my dad."*

Mel sat up. "Whoa. Okay. Let me know what the big guns think."

"It's going to start with curse words, and he knows a lot." Alyla smiled. *"Glad you are safe, Mel. Stay that way."*

"Fuck off!"

Alyla smiled. *"Nice to see you, too, Marko."*

The screen went dark.

Mel knew that a whole bunch of live relays had been used to get that message through so quickly, so Alyla had been waiting for that signal.

Mel looked at the walls. "Station?"

"Yes, Terran?"

"Call me Mel. I don't qualify as a Terran anymore. There is not one fucking person on my world this tall."

"Very well, Mel. You may call me Ves."

"Thank you, Ves. You mentioned that there were rations."

"There is a food centre if you follow the blue light. Marko has already been."

Mel nodded and got up, walking slowly along the wall.

"You are doing very well, Mel. The gravity on the station is set to five times your Terran standard. I applaud your range of motion coming out of the med pod."

Mel paused. "Five times. Wow. Well, it explains why the folks attacking the pod didn't want to come in. Skevarik are a level three. They would have been crawling around."

She walked with an arm on the wall and pushed herself upright now and then. Marko flew ahead of her, and the blue light continued to lead her further into the station.

Despite her knowing that she should be all stressed out, Mel just wanted to see what she could get out of the food machine. Being big burned a lot of calories.

* * * *

Imbolt stared at the com. "They did what?"

"They tried to destroy the delivery vessel, but the vessel stowed Mel in a high-grav station and then used itself as a decoy. The station defended itself after that. I will send you the video."

"Thank you, little star." He watched the delivery unit skim beneath the station, eject the pod, and continue on without pausing. The followers had no idea that the woman was no longer in the delivery unit. The station took the pod in quickly, and the hunters were none the wiser.

"She is all right?"

"She and her cursing bird, but I am going to have to ask Mom why she let a parrot pick the human's colouring."

Imbolt frowned. "Show me."

The visual of the woman with a green crest of hair, blue features and crimson extremities made Imbolt smile. "Oh, I know what those markings are. I need to send a message to the Vendori home world."

"What about the Skevarik?"

"They are banned from getting a Terran in perpetuity, as are the original species. No guardian, no defender. Nothing. Spread this news through surrounding systems."

Alyla frowned. "What did you see when you saw her colouring?"

"Something old and familiar."

"You are old and familiar." His daughter laughed.

"You sound like your mother." He grinned as his fingers tapped messages, and then, the core of him sent a message and waited for a reply.

"She's been an amazing influence. At least I called you first thing."

Imbolt sighed. "Thank you, Alyla."

She chuckled. "You are welcome, Dad. What the hell could they have been thinking?"

"The factions can be divided. A scenario is forming, and it is the only one that is partially understandable."

"What is it?"

"If the male she was compatible with died, they needed a bride for his funeral."

"Holy shit."

"There's your mom again. If they were actually bound, it would be necessary to put her out of her suffering, but as they have never met, it would be for optics. To show he was cared for and a good leader."

"How can having a dead wife make that clear?"

"I have no idea. I would burn out solar systems for your mother, so I am not really a good judge of what is appropriate, but I would do that for her but not to her."

Alyla nodded. "When are you coming home?"

"If I can get this straightened out, in ten days; if not, I will have to remain out here and possibly take a visit to the station."

"Right. Of course. Mel is a priority." She nodded. "I just have one question."

"Yes?"

"Where was the delivery unit for the last six weeks? How did it get so close to the station? How did it communicate with the station?"

Imbolt nodded. "Excellent questions. The queries are out in the air now. We have to wait."

He felt a tapping on his mind and opened his thoughts to the avatar.

Zanicon, I got your query. Is there really such a female at my station?

Imbolt snorted. *Yes, and you are aware of it.*

Am I?

No one gets on that station without your permission, and yet, you have invited an altered Terran in for safety only.

How unusually generous of me.

And she is pigmented like one of your avatars. As in, the avatar you are currently speaking through.

Fascinating. Well, we are busy working on some renovations on one of my system worlds. She is safe where she is. That creature of hers is amusing as well.

You did it on purpose?

She is worth far more than those two idiots could offer her. She has to simply wait until we have time to introduce her to her new worlds.

Stellar avatars are a pain in the ass.

The voice chuckled. *We see so much, and our avatars are both dense and radioactive.*

We'll, dense fits the bill. How long are you going to leave her there?

A few months or years.

Fuck you, you pasty bitch. I am going to come get her now.

You do, and the station will destroy you.

It will destroy my vessel; I will be fine. Imbolt was irritated. *You will not be fine when I catch up with you if you don't agree to at least make contact with her.*

I am making her a lovely home to live in and relax in.

This is a woman of action, a woman who depends on others for equilibrium. She is not the placid type.

Ah, I had not counted on that. Others in this project are placid.

No, they aren't. They have guardian-level strength, others have open minds, another has skin of flame, and another has death as a companion. They are not placid.

My host is intrigued. We will make our way there within thirty days. Acceptable?

Acceptable, but we are watching.

Understood. If she is to be a companion, I will have to make alternate arrangements and get him to control his burn.

That would be appreciated. We are watching the time. We are expecting progress.

Yes, Zanican, I understand.

The connection thinned to a micro connection, and Imbolt-Zanican conferred with each other on the likelihood of Vendor actually going to the station in the next month. Fortunately, from her file, Mel could entertain herself.

* * * *

Mel raced down the court and jumped as she launched the ball into the hoop Ves had set up for her. Marko struck the ball and knocked it away from the hoop, and Mel landed in a crouch. "Damn it, Marko, you are ruining my groove."

"Loser. Try again, dumbass."

Mel huffed, sprinted back to the other side of the court, and then began dribbling and running back down the court. Jumping into the air, she swatted Marko away and got the ball into the hoop.

"Bitch. Smack yourself!"

Mel laughed. "Hah. That's two-two. I am catching up."

The proximity alarm sounded, and she sighed. "I am going to beat you, bird. Don't think this is over."

She lifted her head. "Ves, what's going on?"

"There is a raider vessel, and it is drifting close to me. I am about to destroy it." There was a pause. "There is a life sign."

"Vertical or horizontal?"

"Horizontal and very cold."

Mel looked at Marko. "Scan the ship, and tell me what you find."

Marko settled on Mel's shoulder and started to flap excitedly.

"Marko has detected a Terran life sign. I am detecting Citadel insignia. If I bring it on board, it will be crushed."

Mel paused. "Can I go out?"

"I don't have a suit for you yet."

"Can Marko?"

Marko screeched and flew for the cargo bay.

"Uh, I hope you let her out because it does not look like she is gonna stop."

Ves stated, "I am opening a hole in the screen."

Mel headed for the cargo area where her tube still was and watched through the display that Marko projected as she screamed for entry to the vessel, and the door opened. As the ship rotated, the gouge on the other side of the ship showed that it had seen some rough events, and there was no atmosphere in the vessel.

The sarcophagus-like pod wasn't Alliance issue. The markings on it were written in some kind of marker or pen. It appeared to be pricing.

"Ves, were they selling it?"

"Her. Designation female. Citadel specialist by the insignia on her robes." Ves paused. "If she can be brought inside, I can arrange a lighter gravity for her. You will have to wear a pressure suit. Your body will have difficulty after an extended period of time in lighter gravity without it."

"Great. How long until I get the suit?"

"One has already been prepared in anticipation of your need to walk with your own kind."

"Cool. Where is it?"

Ves paused, and Mel grinned. His pauses were like a deep sigh. "The medical bay. That is where the extruded suit is."

She skipped all the way to the med bay and mentally thanked Marko for her nagging during workouts. Three weeks and three days in and she was moving around like it was her natural habitat.

"Wow. I like the suit."

"Thank you. It is attractive as well as functional."

She grinned and stripped, pulling the shirt with the net and webbing on before pulling on the leggings. The two items nearly met in the middle, and that was good enough for her.

"Activate it. Clip the top to the sides. Press the icon on the front."

There was a distinct hum as the suit powered up. "Wow. Very nice, Ves."

"Thank you, Mel. I gained inspiration from your favourite clothing and crossed it with the need for the compression field. It is powered off your body heat."

"Nice. Lord knows I am hot with all this density involved. Oh. Boots."

"Marko has expressed your interest in them."

She deactivated the suit, put the boots on, and reactivated it.

"You have the hang of it. The gravity field is being reduced to tolerable levels for your species."

"Nice. I do feel a little lighter. When are you bringing the ship in?"

"Now, Mel. You can head back to the hold now."

Mel grinned and started to run through the halls, enjoying the freedom that came with the suit. She felt like she was running in hero wind.

CHAPTER THREE

Mel watched the vessel approach and be slowly settled onto the floor of the cargo hold.

Marko flew out and settled on Mel's shoulder. She was given a quick look into everything Marko saw via an implant Ves had installed.

"Well, Marko, it looks like we have company. Are you adjusting to the lighter gravity?"

"Shut up, bitch!"

"Thought so." She scratched Marko under the chin as the ship went through a decontamination protocol. Marko hadn't touched anything, and there wasn't any atmosphere.

Bots rolled forward and opened the ship, splitting it and then rolling the container with the Terran in it out onto the deck.

"I will wake her. You may want to appear smaller, Mel."

Mel frowned. "What? Oh."

"Get on your knees, cunt."

"Really, Marko? That is a little crass, even for you."

Marko ruffled her feathers and settled in.

They watched the bots start the waking protocol.

The container began to show glyphs that indicated it was warming the occupant. Mel crouched and waited. The lid exploded upward, and a woman with glowing fists and a wild expression hovered above it, one glowing fist pointed at Mel.

Mel grinned. She said in English, "Well, fuck me."

The woman paused. "Say that again."

"No, but I can say I love your outfit and would kill to meet your tailor. All I get is industrial spandex. My name is Mel. I am one of the Terran Resets. You are..."

"Norel. Specialist Annabelle Norel. What year is it?"

"Ves? What year is it?"

"Annabelle Norel disappeared sixteen years ago, according to Citadel records. I have been in contact with them, but they wish to speak to her."

She sank and sat on the pod. "Sixteen years. Oh, god."

Annabelle put her face in her hands and started to sob.

"Be quiet, bitch!"

Annabelle lifted her head in astonishment.

"Marko, not helpful. Sorry, Specialist Norel. My parrot was part of my volunteer agreement, but I didn't expect to run into too many others who spoke English."

Ves said, "Mel, Marko now speaks nineteen languages, all of the Nyal Imperium."

"Aw, fuck. That isn't going to be awkward at all."

Annabelle chuckled. "So, you are actually human."

"I was. My alterations were a little more physical and less psychic. Marko was adjusted to fit my new size. I was supposed to be a mail-order bride of sorts, but no one wants me, and then Marko is claiming that she selected my current colouration. I am the same colours she used to be."

Marko fluffed herself up.

"If you would like to go to the com room, I can take you there, but don't freak out if I stand up."

"I can't promise," Annabelle said.

Mel shrugged and stood. Annabelle gasped. "Holy shit!"

Mel smiled. "Yeah. Big girl problems. So, come this way, please."

She led the way through the ship, and Annabelle flew behind her. "So, were you in training to be a guardian?"

"No. I was a hired bodyguard, but my last client sold me. It got ugly for a year, and then, it was decided that I was too much trouble. They passed me around and finally sold me with my spotted history over and over again."

"I just want to give you a hug."

"That would be good. The first year was... horrifying."

"Oh. Shit."

"String 'em up. Cut their balls off."

Annabelle chuckled weakly. "So, the parrot understands?"

"The parrot and I are linked, so I can see what she sees if I try, and when we were talking, I had images come to mind, and Marko interpreted those."

"Marko? I thought you said it was a girl."

"Marko was named decades before she came into my care, and I had no reason to believe it wasn't a he." Mel grinned even though Annabelle was behind her. "That is also where the language was acquired."

"Filthy bitch!"

Annabelle chuckled. "Got it."

They entered the com room, and Ves was already dialling the Citadel. Annabelle perched in the Mel-sized chair and waited.

"So, how far out are we?"

"The ass end of the Nyal Imperium. This station was set for a gravitational force of five. Like Jupiter plus."

Annabelle looked around warily. "What happened?"

"Ves welcomed a guest, so I am in a suit to keep me together. Marko doesn't care because she has transcended protein-based feathers."

Ves spoke. "The ladies insisted that we bring you on board."

Annabelle swallowed. "That is the station?"

"Yeah. Sounds kind of sexy, but he's too much man for me."

Ves clicked open his mic, paused, and said, "Mel, you have to stop flirting with me."

"Why? It's a fun hobby." She didn't mention that her food had gotten exponentially better since she started.

The screen sprang to life, and a Citadel logo filled the screen.

A being with flared-out ears and a soft-green complexion filled the viewer. "*Specialist Norel, you are found and very much alive.*"

Annabelle nodded and leaned forward. "Yes, and I am eager to get back to the Citadel."

"*Impossible. Your debt load for search efforts is extreme. Unless you can come up with seven hundred fifty thousand credits, we can't take you back."*

Mel blinked and whispered, "Ves, how much did Norel make in a year?"

"Fifty thousand."

"Fuck me."

Annabelle's eyes were streaming. "You don't understand what happened. What they did to me."

"We understand that you were abducted while on duty, which meant we had to send a replacement. Then, there were the efforts to locate you and the reward offered."

Mel paused and whispered to Ves, "See if the reward is still standing."

There was a pause and a whisper, "Yes. To be collected by delivering her alive and well to the Citadel or any Sector Guard outpost, even Guardian bases."

"Who pays more?"

"Guardian bases. The Imperial court supplements them. They are paying over a million for her safe return."

Mel chuckled. "Neat. Ves, are there any functioning vessels on this station? Something that fits me?"

"Why do you ask, Mel?"

"Because Annabelle wants a home and deserves to be

somewhere she feels safe. So, we bring her to a safe place, collect the reward, pay off the Citadel, and she is a free woman."

"Unusual train of thought. You want to free her."

"Once we pay off the Citadel, she will be free to choose her path, and with her basic skills, she can take a position in planetary defense or in law enforcement."

Mel watched as Marko waddled up to the seat where Annabelle was begging.

"Fuck off, you poxy cow!" Marko slammed her beak down on the console, and the connection was cut.

Annabelle looked at the bird, and Marko looked back at her. *"Ask the tall bitch!"*

Annabelle looked around, smiling through her tears. "That would be you?"

"That would be me. Ves is making a few calls, and we are going to get you a reward for being alive and a place that you can call home and get some healing."

She stood up. "Come on, we are going to discuss my plans over food. You have been out for a while, and Ves does a particularly nice herb soup. Hope on, Marko. Time for snackies."

The bird thudded to her shoulder, and Annabelle stepped

toward her. Their little trio headed off for some food.

Mel explained her musings and left Ves to work on getting them some transport.

"So, you just asked the station for transport?"

"Yeah. I mean, he's a space station. He has to have a vehicle stashed somewhere, and I can't image creeping around in a standard shuttle. I am kinda hard to fit in the back seat." She ordered food for all three of them, and since Marko's came out first, she set her bird on the perch near the dispenser and put the bowls in the loops included on the perch. Marko hopped around happily and nibbled away.

"Were the stands and such always here?"

Mel laughed. "No. Marko started making demands as soon as she was in here. Getting me out was one, and making herself comfortable and getting snacks was another. I have a bedroom, the common spaces, and a gym to work out in, and Marko has everything else: perches in every room and a supply of snacks she can summon at will, but she prefers to have them summoned for her cuz she's a pretty girl."

Annabelle looked at the tray that Mel brought her. "Wow. This is a lot."

"I will eat anything you don't. I require three of these trays as I need more stuff." She smiled. "They don't make fruit with extra density."

Annabelle asked, "You really mean to collect a ransom for me?"

"A reward. I will collect the reward, pay your bill at the Citadel, and then you have a number of places that will do wonders at helping you work through your trauma and become more yourself again."

Annabelle blinked. "What? I thought you wanted the money."

"What would I do with money? I can't settle on any world with normal gravity. I have no idea what species I am compatible with, and I have my bird for company. I am good with Vendari Station. It's quiet. I can exercise without someone staring at my ass, and Lunar Base sent me all of my favourite music. I am really content here." She smiled. "I know I look weird, but I really want you to be somewhere and happy. I... know what that kind of trauma can do to a person, and to experience it more than once would send you into a spiral. So, Ves has been looking at Guardian bases and spas since they are closer, and a few look likely as good places to get yourself therapy, healing, and decide on your next move."

"Just like that?" Annabelle was sipping at her green soup.

"This is really good. My compliments, Ves."

"Thank you, Specialist. Marko and Mel are honest critics."

Mel chuckled and began to eat in earnest.

Annabelle smiled and continued with the soup, moving on to the bread and then the other dishes. "Why did you turn the gravity down?"

"Because I don't want my first human contact out here to be in flatland. I need way more gravity than you to function normally."

She got up and picked up her second tray, putting the firsts in the cleaning slot.

Mel sat and continued eating. "I spend about an hour and a half per day just consuming food. None of the denser offerings sit well with me. Apparently, there are fruits to help with that, but we don't have them here."

"Well, if this works, I will help you do high-gravity research."

"Thanks."

Ves said, "I can tell her what she needs to know."

Mel snorted. "But, sometimes, I am in the middle of things before I think to ask."

"Right. I will have a vessel prepared for you in twenty hours. I have received several answers to our query, but you will be forwarded the reward, and Specialist Norel will have a place to recover on Rai."

"Why is that familiar?"

A display projected in front of her and Annabelle as an aerial shot went in on a lush green world with minimal tech. When the population was highlighted, Annabelle blinked. "Is that..."

"It looks like a combo of Admaryn and a very powerful species. The pointy ears give the elves away every time. There are two Terrans on the surface, now related by marriage, more or less. One is a Reset like I am, and the other is from the first wave." The women were highlighted in what were more kimono-like clothing than anything else. Each was standing with a local that had the stamp of the Guardians, and Fade had four children, all grown and standing near her.

"Wow. Those are tall kids." Annabelle stared. "I have seen a few Terrans with kids but never with them already grown."

"The file says that Fade's children are in Guardian training for planetary and extra-planetary defense."

"What file?"

"Uh... Ves, are you doing that thing again?"

"I am."

"Oh, Annabelle, you are seeing the image, and I am getting

the intel from the files that Ves has accessed. It's something he's been practicing."

"How?"

"Oh, I was lying on the deck, and before they woke me up, he jacked my brain full of implants. It's an attractive arrangement on a scan. Even Marko thinks so because two of them are hers, but the ones between us are a little awkward and at will."

Annabelle blinked. "They did what?"

"Ves needed to communicate with me, and I didn't speak his language, so he had to download mine from my mind. By the time I woke up, I had a headache but was speaking what I thought was English but turned out to be Vendari."

Ves spoke. "It was necessary. She was not rising, and I could not communicate with her. Marko suggested direct intervention, so I downloaded a map of a Terran brain, scaled it up, and put in the filaments. They have mostly absorbed already."

Annabelle cleared her throat. "Do you think they will let me stay on Rai?"

"They do have a retreat there that the other Reset is working on, and they specialize in getting Guardians the help they need and finding out what their heart needs."

Annabelle paused. "That is what she does. She helps them open up what their soul wants."

"That is what they say. So, do you consider Rai a possible destination?"

Annabelle smiled. "I think it's a good start. I am already wearing the robe."

They giggled and finished their meals, talking about Earth, changes, and society moving forward as one in slow starts and jerks. Some countries still tried to flail around and impose their will, but that faded quickly when the benefits of the Alliance were withdrawn from all warring nations. Minerva may not be acknowledged by all, but Gaia was making her presence felt. Having a Lunar Base that no government could claim was also a handy thing. It kept the Alliance moving along smoothly.

Ves directed Annabelle to her quarters where a terminal had been set up, and Alyla's face was bright and smiling, her monochromatic patterns bright and her grin wide.

"Hi, Annabelle. My name is Alyla, and you have met my mother, or maybe her alter ego, Recruiter Norz. She has things to work on, but she asked me to talk to you as long as you need until you are comfortable, no matter the topic."

Annabelle walked to the chair and took a seat. Mel listened

to her start the conversation, and then she left the Terran to her conversation.

Mel went to bed, and Marko came in and chortled on her covered perch. She didn't need the darkness, but she liked to be close when Mel slept.

Mel had one question for Ves regarding her companion, and the answer was that processed foods became fuel and made Marko a self-contained unit that needed fuel for an input. No messy base of the stands aside from cracked seeds and splashed water.

Mel settled for bed in her bodysuit; a solar shower was fine for the small amount of time Annabelle would be with her.

She muttered, "Whatever kind of vessel you are cooking up, Ves, can you give me instructions on how to fly it?"

"It will not be necessary. I am going with you."

"What?"

"I am sending myself, bots, and a link to this station with you so that you are not unguarded."

"Why is that a thing?"

"Because your people are worried about you and wish to make sure that you are protected. I will protect you."

"You are a space station."

"Who knows how to fly a ship."

"Ouch. Mean. So, do you have a robot or something?"

He chuckled. "Or something. Rest. Relax. Tomorrow, you will get to see the stars."

"I can see them from the station." She yawned and settled to try and sleep.

"Not like this. The Rai system is particularly beautiful. You and Marko will have fun."

"Why are you so concerned about us enjoying ourselves?"

"I am concerned that you and your companion have not seen the best of what the heavy worlds have to offer. Rai is not a heavy world, but it is near several. They see your people often."

"My people?" She yawned again.

"Heavy worlders. Rest now. I have to fit the ship with rations."

She chuckled and closed her eyes. The light in her room dimmed, and she heard, *"Night, you cow."*

"Back atcha, Marko."

CHAPTER FOUR

Mel had breakfast with Marko, and Annabelle walked in, looking around. "This place is huge."

Mel grinned. "You know, your house and your pets start to look like you after a while."

Annabelle chuckled. "So, you turned into Marko?"

"Clever. Breakfast is set up. Just press the big blue button."

"Thank you."

Annabelle pressed the button, and there was a loud chime as the dispenser sent out the tray.

Mel kept eating as Annabelle staggered over. She grinned as the tray slid onto the table, and Annabelle hopped up onto the chair. "I feel like a fucking toddler."

Mel shrugged and kept eating. "Eat your oatmeal like a

good girl, and maybe, we can go for a walk when you are done. Or do you need a nap?"

"Hah. You are funny. You know I can see up your nose, right?"

Mel spluttered and put a hand over her face as the aforementioned nose provided an exit for her breakfast. "Ow."

Annabelle laughed and snorted as she watched Mel struggle.

It was the start of an interesting day.

The ship was astonishing. It looked like a manta ray but was tall enough for Mel to move in easily.

Ves said, "Clothing has been created for both of you and is in your quarters. Food for Marko and rations for both of you for a minimum of three months, and a pressure tank is available for Mel when she needs a break from the suits she's wearing. Are you ready to travel?"

Mel looked around and found her bed ready for her long limbs. "Yeah, I guess we are. Are we going straight to Rai?"

"The Alliance has requested that we make a short stop at Veth so you can meet another Reset."

"Veth? Who is the Terran?"

"Identity is Liona Kix, mate to Neevath, the Drai Avatar."

"Wow. They are telling you everything."

Ves chuckled. "I am a trustworthy station. Now, everyone to their takeoff seats. We are going to leave the station."

Marko flapped to the front of the vessel with its twenty-foot ceilings and settled in a half-egg pod lined with some kind of soft backing.

Mel found the large chair, and Annabelle set herself in the smaller one. They buckled in, and Ves said, "Route currently is Veth, Rai, and Possit Two."

Mel paused. "Why stop at all those places?"

Ves chuckled. "They all have a Reset Terran."

Mel grinned. "Freakier than me?"

"That is why we are stopping at Veth first. Liona has had extreme changes, and it will do you good to see someone who has settled into her transformation."

Mel asked, "Alyla's suggestion?"

"She is wise for a young woman. The permissions have been obtained, and we are underway. First planet will be reached in twenty-six hours."

"I didn't realize we were moving. That was smooth, Ves."

Ves chuckled. "Thank you. I love what I do."

Mel grinned and asked, "Can we walk around?"

"Certainly. I will announce dinner. For now, explore, but don't try to use the exits."

"Funny."

There was a chuckle, and Marko nestled into her little safety egg, tucked her beak under her arm, and had a comfy nap.

Mel unsnapped her harness and got up, going exploring beyond her bedroom. She found the food dispensers, the recreation room, a gym, and a cargo area.

She looked at the cargo area, and something was being built. "Ves, what's that?"

"You will need a shuttle, which I will also fly. I do not trust your attention span with atmospheric flight," Ves murmured.

"Mean. Accurate but mean."

She looked at the gym and said, "Will you call me for lunch?"

"Of course."

She headed into the gym, set everything for her new levels, and got to work. She was still growing, but it had slowed down. It seemed that she didn't have a partner on the horizon, so the reproductive clause in the contract was going to burn out in three years.

Whatever she was going to do after that was probably

going to be odd. She had never done the predictable thing.

She took a break and sat, thinking about her brother and his heart attack. He had been older than his years and ignored his kids. Giving her house and accounts to her niece had just felt like the right thing. Make up for family failings.

She leaned forward and held her head in her hands. The reset didn't undo her life; it just meant that she could choose not to make the same mistakes again. Of course, she could still make the same mistakes, but right now, Mel was choosing the other path.

"Mel, are you all right?"

"I am old, I am an unidentifiable species, and I just bench-pressed more than my SUV. I am coming to grips with my dwindling humanity." She snorted. "Hell, I think I am not too far from weighing more than my SUV." She looked at Annabelle. "How is your day going?"

"Uh, pretty benign compared to that. Thanks for doing this. For asking Ves to do this."

"I need to thank him. I think I just told him what I wanted, and he made it happen."

Annabelle chuckled. "That's what I guessed. You made him bring me in, too."

"Um. Yeah. Pretty sure I was considering going out after

you." Mel scratched the back of her neck.

"How would that have worked out? Not a clue. Probably not well."

Ves spoke, "I would have put a tether on you, and you would have had five minutes to find a handhold before I reeled you in."

"I can hold my breath that long?"

"No, but you are dense enough not to lose all your body heat immediately."

"Thanks. That is what all the ladies like to hear."

Annabelle chuckled.

Ves sighed. "You have been remade for a Vendari."

"According to your records, all the Vendari are dead, so that is like saying I am the only girl in the cemetery."

"Arrangements have been made, Mel. Do not worry."

Mel snorted. "I can worry if I want to. Marko even has started calling me a giant freak. It's working on my nerves. And I can put up with her calling me a lot of crap."

Ves clicked on and paused, "You are speaking the truth. Your companion has been blunt about her opinions."

Annabelle said, "It isn't that bad. A few of the male Citadel members are eight feet tall."

"Based on the gap in my clothing, I grew four inches

overnight... again. I don't know when it's going to stop, and I feel like seeing if my pituitary gland can be extracted."

Ves said, "No, your maximum height will be achieved in a quarter of a metre."

She grunted and nodded.

"You are going to get a foot taller?" Annabelle put her hand on Mel's shoulder.

"Apparently. Wonderful." Her head stayed in her hands. Mel sighed and said, "I am interfering with your workout. You should go, and do what you want."

She smiled and stood, swaying a little.

"I don't think this equipment will fit me. I am not trying to hustle you out of here."

"No, it's fine. I need to go to my room."

"Is there anything I can do?"

"No. If I didn't know better, I would say this is PMS. I am all dark and moody."

"Aren't you neutralized?"

"Apparently not. Delightful. If anything would make me think twice about the reset aside from the height, it would be a period. I feel so lucky." She got up. "I am going to check the med scanner just to confirm."

Annabelle stood there, and Mel could hear talking voices

behind her, so Ves was asking what the issue was.

She went into the medical space and settled into the scanner, keying in what she wanted to check. Mel lay back and waited for the scan, and when it finished, she looked at the results. "Of course."

She was a day away from a period, and hers had never been gentle and polite.

"What are you seeing, Mel?"

"A menstrual cycle is going to knock me on my ass tomorrow. I thought I had a suppressor shot."

"It was insufficient for your physical situation."

"Oh. Delightful."

"What do you need?"

"A dark room, chocolate, and a warm blanket," she muttered. "Maybe a sad movie."

"Will you be able to meet with the avatar of Veth?"

"Probably. Why would I need to?"

"Because his mate is another Reset."

She felt her eyes burning as negative emotions swamped her. "I will be ready at the time. Just give me some quiet time."

"I am worried."

"It will be fine, Ves. Tomorrow, the mood will turn to pain, and that is easier to deal with." She chuckled. "And then we have a reprieve, and it will happen again."

"Oh. I will contact Zanican for advice."

She snorted and headed for her room. "Contact whomever you like. I am going to lie down."

Mel felt the internal self-pity hitting her in waves, and she curled up under her light sheet and turned the lights down.

"Mel, it is time for your meal." Ves's voice was calm.

"Not hungry."

"You are still growing. You need to eat."

She mumbled, "If I stop eating, will I stop growing?"

"No, but you will end up in medical jacked full of supplements, and you will miss your chance to walk on an alien world. The Veth don't generally allow visitors, but I think this will be good for you. They have made an exception for the two Terrans on board."

"Annabelle and Marko?"

"Just get up, Mel. I know you feel terrible, dark, and weighed down, but it will pass." Ves paused. "Please."

She groaned and sat up. She was hungry, thirsty, and dark. She felt the darkness in her all the way. The thin sheet flipped to one side, and she slowly stood. The first thing she learned was that standing fast was a tremendous error.

Mel put on her shoes and walked to the food dispenser area. Annabelle was sitting, and Marko was shifting nervously on her perch. Mel went to the dispenser, got her trays, and sat at the table. She started to eat. "How long was I out?"

Ves said, "Eighteen hours. How are you?"

"Awake."

Annabelle smiled. "Ready to see your first alien world?"

"Sure." She ate the food and bused her table.

A med bot trundled in, and a cuff snapped around her arm to hold her as an injector pressed to her abdomen, and then, it did it again on the other side, through her suit.

"Ow. What was that?"

"Hormones. Suggested by your avatar. They should assist so that you are able to interact with the avatar and his mate."

Mel grunted. "Great. I will be in the lav until we land."

Ves indicated, "That was mentioned. We are in the system and will be near the station in two hours."

"Great. I will try and purge quickly."

She headed for her bathroom quietly, stripped out of her suit completely and proceeded to get very ill for an hour and a half. Progesterone was a bitch.

When she was dressed in a dark silver compression set and

had brushed her hair out, she was feeling a bit better, and the mood was lifting slightly.

When they met in the cargo hold, Marko sat on her shoulder and rubbed her head and beak against Mel's temple.

"Don't suck up to me. You know what you said."

"Oopsie daisy!"

Annabelle jolted. "Wait, she's fully sentient?"

"Oh, yes. Her linguistic skills are that of a four-year-old, but her cognition was boosted a lot when she went from green to silver."

Annabelle looked at the silver parrot in astonishment. "I thought..."

"She's not just a mimic. Never has been. No one is ever listening to the meaning behind her cursing. They just listen and laugh."

"Shut up, bitch." Marko rubbed heads with her. The words were softer.

Annabelle chuckled. "She's saying you are always listening."

"You are translating. Nice." She chuckled.

Annabelle asked, "How are you feeling?"

"Empty. Hollow. Blanked out. But, otherwise, delightful. Hormones are rough. Going insane from the inside out. It hit me hard. I was out of practice."

Annabelle smiled. "Suppressor shots are lovely, but I guess they have to wait until you stop growing to give them to you."

Mel nodded. "Yeah, I was firmly in menopause when the avatar came to get me. Riddled with lung cancer. Not a lot of action on my side."

Ves spoke cautiously. "You are ready to land on Veth?"

"I am ready to get in the shuttle. Landing is up to you, Ves."

He seemed relieved. "Correct. Now, please get into the shuttle and strap in."

"Strap on! Everybody, strap on!" Marko chortled.

"Oy." Mel headed into the shuttle and smiled that it was made for her height and a little bit more.

They settled in, and the door sealed and pressurized. The vessel lifted off and glided through the energy screen that kept the station free of debris.

Annabelle smiled. "I love the idea of Resets."

"Do you?"

"Yes. There were so many applications for the original volunteers that I don't doubt some of you were left behind."

Melora chuckled. "Is that what you think? I was shipped off to a war zone when my acceptance letter arrived. Another lady was too old when she applied. She was already outside the limits. We weren't left behind; our applications were put on hold until there was a program to take us. Or until we were on the fine edge of death. Alyla told me all about it."

Annabelle asked, "Who is Alyla again?"

"The daughter of Minerva-Gaia, the avatar of Earth, and a black hole named Imbolt-Zanican. Alyla is great. Her dad is running most of the Resets to their new placements, but no one was headed out this way, so I was delivered by unmanned transport."

Annabelle blinked. "Oh, right."

Marko squawked, *"Dark and cold."*

Mel shrugged as they could see the stars ahead of them and the station in the distance.

Marko muttered, *"Make friends. Influence people."*

Mel chuckled. "Yes, Mom."

Ves stated, "We have bypass authorization for the surface. The lady of Veth is waiting to greet you."

He flew next to the station slowly. There was a chime, and then they began to move toward the surface.

Mel slowly exhaled and inhaled as they jostled through the entry to the atmosphere. They began a controlled descent, and Mel's eyes widened as she saw a dragon in brick-red and gold flying next to them. Ves brought them down in a meadow near a small settlement, and the dragon settled next to them.

There was the hiss of atmosphere as the rear of the shuttle opened so Mel could get out. Annabelle stepped out in her Citadel robes as Marko jumped onto Mel's shoulder. They walked out, and the dragon opened a claw, showing a golden woman with dragon wings that moved into a familiar position that made Mel smile.

Annabelle rushed to the Drai female and introduced herself.

"Lady, it is an honour to greet you."

The woman arched her brow and looked at Annabelle. "You are not the Reset."

"No. I am a volunteer who was kept in stasis."

"I am glad you have survived, but I need to speak to the... holy shit."

Mel walked up and crossed her arms. "Goliath was my favourite."

The lady grinned. "Hello, I am Liona. Full-body cancer patient."

"I am Melora, Mel. Lung cancer and emphysema from secondhand exposure in the service industry. This is Marko. I think she has a crush on your husband."

"Hot damn, that's a tall drink of water." Marko chortled.

The dragon gave her a look.

Mel launched her. "Go make friends, but he walks on two legs, and the beast might be hungry, so stay out of snapping distance and speak Drai or common."

Liona chuckled. "I have never seen... is the bird Terran as well?"

"She is. She has been remade a bit." Mel made a face. "Should I sit or kneel?"

"I am good. Neevath isn't as tall as you, but he's about your chin height. As long as you aren't trying to makeout with me, I am fine."

Liona stretched and flexed her wings, unhooking them at the collar and stretching. "So, we are both majorly physically altered."

She turned to Annabelle. "I am sorry, dear. I don't mean to be rude, but I don't have long to speak to Mel. She needs more intervention than you."

"Intervention?"

Liona smiled. "You were eased into your change. I had it explained the whole way, and Neevath took over the details, mostly. He was very excited about the wings. She was made for a partner that hasn't manifested. She's experiencing something none of our kind have, and there is little time to enjoy it. She has been frantically adapting and doing what she could to keep on top of the changes."

Annabelle cleared her throat. "I am going to go to the village for a bit. Ves will recall me when it's time."

"Excellent, dear, there are Guardians in town today. You might be able to talk shop with them."

Mel was concerned. "Stick to the ladies. Men in the Nyal Imperium are a little forward, and you still need some help."

Annabelle frowned. "I can manage."

Mel looked at Liona. "So, you sound like you have been briefed."

"I have. Zanican is freaked out that you are out here in this condition. No one has seen a Vendari in centuries, and the other species wouldn't dare mess with you."

"Ah. Right. So, armour-plated for convenience."

"Social strictures. Vendari set themselves up as gods in a number of systems. How did you end up with this?"

"No idea. I was being changed into a Skevarik but woke up coloured like Marko's before picture."

"Ah. Well, at least you don't have to learn about wings and how they work. My wing thumbs used to tangle a lot, and Neevath would just come up to me and unhook them with a smile. How long has your transformation been so far?"

"Um, three or four months? I had to do most of it at the Lunar Base, and then I was launched in an unmanned vessel. I can't seem to get the hang of moving. I feel slower every day."

"Dance. Learn to dance. Move, and every day it will be easier. You need to keep in touch with how far your limbs stretch and how hard it is to change direction. If your mate isn't around to help, you are going to have to master your own body and try to have fun. You need to find fun in your own body again. I know it has been a while. Possibly decades are involved. Move until your limbs are under your control and you feel comfortable in your own skin. It is what kids literally do. They wiggle around and learn how their bodies move. That is your assignment."

Mel smiled. "So, I should wiggle?"

"You should accept that this is your body, and you need to control it."

Mel nodded and looked at Marko and the dragon. The bird was squawking and had her arms wide as if she was telling the dragon a story. The dragon was looking at her and nodding intently.

"Aw, she made a friend." Mel chuckled.

Liona looked and blinked. "Wow. She's talking to Veth."

"How can you tell?"

"The eyes. The eyes change when a celestial being is talking through their avatar."

Mel blinked. "Are there a lot of them?"

"It's a one-in-a-thousand situation. It is far rarer to find a Drai out and away from their world. To find a female with Drai wings... unheard of. The Reset Project is having fun with this."

"Well, someone is. I am having my first period in twenty-five years and am slightly miserable. Ves loaded me full of hormones to balance me out, but I still have that gloom-and-doom thing going on. I wish that I was less moody meeting another Reset."

Liona smiled. "Don't worry about it. I got a Drai, and your mate has yet to make themselves known. I can only imagine the frustration. If I had to go through growing the wings without him, I would have gone insane."

"I had Marko, and Ves is a good sport."

"Ves?"

"Vendari Station. That is where I woke up. The consciousness of the station has been making equipment and getting rations and snacks for us."

Annabelle smiled as she walked by with arms loaded with fruit. "Just passing through. I'll be back."

Mel looked and blinked. "What the hell?"

Liona laughed. "Do you have internal coms?"

"Yeah."

"Did Annabelle get one?"

Liona chuckled. "Someone is telling her to get the breeding fruit."

"Breeding... No fucking way."

"It is a soother for hormonal upsets. You might be able to keep blues at bay with one of those. If the vendors hadn't shared it with me, Veth was going to destroy every single crop on the planet. They would wither and die because they wouldn't let me try one."

"Good spouse."

"Oh, yeah. So, what's the deal with the suit?"

"Oh, I am set for heavy grav now, so it keeps me from losing molecular density."

Liona's eyes went wide. "So, are you super strong?"

"Dunno."

"Can you jump over tall buildings in a single bound?"

"Not a clue. This is the first atmosphere I have been in since I passed seven foot five."

"You are moving so calmly."

"I don't bounce out of vessels. I get the feeling at my current size that it might cause some kind of armed response."

Liona blinked. "Oh... right."

Mel smiled and watched Annabelle walk back to the village with a grin on her face.

"She's having fun."

Liona smiled. "I think this is what Veth was doing earlier. He ordered... things for you."

"Me?"

"Yes."

"Why?"

"Someone is almost ready to court you."

"What?"

"Sure. This is how they do things when you have established hobbies. Food, clothing, making you comfortable, and then the seduction. Frankly, by the time they get that far, you are just willing to pin them down and jump them. No social mores here, no other Terrans making faces at you for falling in love with another species. No guys calling you unpleasant names. If you want to, and they want to, go for it, but make sure you understand their social structure. For example, there is one species that has a trigger word. Hospitality. If you ask them for hospitality and they accept the responsibility, they are duty bound to make you cum until you pass out and your body has no need."

"I can't find any information on the Vendari. I don't know if Ves is missing the info or hiding it from me."

"Probably hiding it." She sighed. "The Vendari were a little on the brutal side from what Neevath has told me."

"So, they had a reputation."

"They did, which is why the planets and celestial bodies got together and exterminated them, diluting their population with others until they were effectively eradicated. It was about five thousand years or so ago, and the Vendari are kind of the boogeyman species now."

"Wait, were they always so tall and heavy?"

Liona sighed. "No, I think that was the consolation that they agreed to for Vendar. He needed a female, and they had to make you unable to be happy on any other worlds."

"So, they put a tether on me. I have to wear the reinforcement and live in heavy grav, so no friends for me."

She nodded.

"Well, Annabelle is with you, and you are here now."

"And if my suit blows, I start coming apart." Mel rubbed

her forehead. "And the station has to be on light gravity for her to be there, so I can't even change clothing without my body feeling really weird with things on light."

Liona touched her arm. "I am sorry."

Mel nodded. "I wish you and your pregnancy all the best. Congratulations on the next generation."

Liona looked down. "I am not even showing yet. How did you know?"

"I can hear the heartbeats. Big slow for you and rapid hamster for the baby."

Annabelle walked by with more armloads of fruit. "Ves says we can go now."

Liona frowned. "So soon?"

"Yes. We are taking Annabelle to Rai. She needs therapy and someone to look after her for a while."

"Why?"

"Confinement, torture, and sexual assault before being told that the Citadel needs their money back before she can get treatment."

"Oh, shit."

"Yeah. Well, it was nice meeting you, Liona. I wish you a lovely life and prosperous union."

"Um, I want to hug you." Liona fidgeted.

"I will be careful." Mel leaned down, and Liona wrapped her arms around Mel's neck.

The whisper, "Just give it time; you aren't done yet," made Mel blink. She patted Liona's back carefully, and when the small woman let her go, she straightened.

Annabelle looked at her and said, "Are you ready?"

Mel lifted her hand, and Marko squawked and flew to her wrist, and then she sidestepped up to her shoulder. Marko looked at Liona. *"Bye, bitch!"*

Liona laughed, and Mel headed back to the ship with her buddy riding high.

They settled in, strapped in, and Ves lifted off. On to Rai.

CHAPTER FIVE

Back on the larger ship and on the way to Rai, Mel sat in her quarters and activated the com.

"Ves, I want to know about the Vendari."

"No."

"What do you mean no?"

"I mean that the people known as the Vendari were nasty, cruel, and brutish, and you don't need to know about them."

Mel paused. "So, you know why I am here."

"Yes, Mel."

"Why am I here?"

"Vendar received permission to try again." Ves paused. "Vendar was delighted to hear from the Reset Project. When they learned that you were already halfway to a Vendari transformation, it was—as you say—a no-brainer. So, they paid to complete your transformation, and it was executed on the station."

"Got it. So, the Skevarik?"

"Tried to steal you when they realized their chance for you had been outbid."

"Which is why they tried to blow me out of the sky."

"They are sore losers."

"And they harbour resentments against the Vendari."

"And yet, they didn't come onto the station." There was a smug and innocent note in the voice.

"Because you have the gravity so high, they would get squashed. Now, honestly, how much gravity do I actually need for survival?"

Ves paused. "Two gravitational forces. You can be adapted for two gravitational forces."

"That is what I thought. This body has felt so weird."

There was another pause. "I am sorry. You should have had help adapting, but there were issues of logistics."

"Yes, I am sure that will make me feel better about the situation."

She sat back. "Does Imbolt know about this? Alyla?"

"The celestial consciousness knows; their daughter does not."

"Okay, that is better. I am going to have a chat with Gaia about this. I am pretty sure that Minerva is going to be pissed as well."

"You are going to tell them?"

"I am a daughter of Gaia. She held my hand and told me everything would be all right. It is not all right. I am alone, and I am scared, and if it weren't for Marko, I would be inconsolable."

"Is this a hormone problem?"

"It doesn't help, but instead of making me mad, it just makes me sad." She rubbed the back of her neck.

"I do not wish you to be sad."

"I don't either, but here we are." She sighed. "I am going to the gym."

"We will be at Rai in two days. You will need to go for an interview on the station."

"Why?"

"Customs check. They want to make sure you aren't going to disappear into the population. You also have to explain how you came to be in possession of a lost Citadel member."

"Oh. Right. I will practice being calm with a polite smile."

Mel headed to the gym, and without invoking Ves, she dialled up some music and decided to give Liona's advice a try. She moved to the mats, started to slide her feet, and moved slowly in dance patterns that she remembered from her misspent youth. When the ethnicity of the music shifted, Mel began to rock her hips while keeping her upper body still. That was tricky, but her balance felt better after she had moved around to the music.

When the classic ballet started up, she tried a pirouette and staggered to catch her balance, but she did it again and again until she could spin.

It was a solid hour later, but the endorphins had started doing their work, and Mel felt herself smiling. She felt lighter as well. She knew how far she could spin without hitting the walls, and that bit of physical competence made her feel good. She was less clumsy after one hour, but she was going to feel it in the morning.

Marko flew toward her and dropped one of the fruits Annabelle had brought on board. *"Eat it, bitch."*

Mel sniffed it and took a bite. It was a cross between dragon fruit and passion fruit to her senses. It tasted nice.

She was in better spirits, and the fruit was boosting her mood tremendously. She returned to the common area and smiled at Annabelle, talking to the retired guardian of Rai who managed the retreat. A room would be waiting as soon as Annabelle arrived, and she could begin treatment with the local therapists at the retreat.

Mel smiled. Annabelle looked hopeful, and that was a very good thing.

Annabelle glanced her way and smiled wide. "Lady Ageka, this is my friend, Melora. She and I are the same species."

Mel walked into view of the camera. "Good day to you, Lady."

The shock was obvious. "*You are the same species?*"

Mel nodded. "I am from the same program that made your Lady Kyna."

"*Snow bunny? You are the same as her?*"

"Different medical conditions but same general result. I don't look like Annabelle here. She is what our species most looks like in height and body type. Pigments vary wildly."

Ageka looked at her carefully. "*Are you coming for an evening?*"

"No, ma'am. I don't think I would fit in at the retreat."

"*Are you sure? I think you could benefit from a good soak, maybe a solid massage.*"

Mel chuckled. "I don't think I fit most of your equipment and certainly not your personnel."

"Well, consider it. Send us your measurements so that we can have materials on hand to make a robe for the retreat. We already have Annabelle's measurements."

"My measurements are changing, so it is difficult to guess where they will be in a few days."

Ageka nodded. "Fine, but send them anyway. I will put authorization for landing in your vessel through to the station. A guardian may come on board to accompany you to the surface, and any deviation from your landing site will be met with aggression. Do you understand?"

Mel asked, "Ves?"

"Yes, absolutely. We will comply with all stated zones."

Ageka nodded. "Good. We don't normally allow foreign vessels on our soil, but we have been told it is considered a medical device for you."

Mel nodded. "You are not wrong. I am completely dependent on the vessel and the mind that drives it."

Ageka nodded again. "I will put the authorizations through. I look forward to meeting you and seeing if you are as tall as you look."

"I am. Do not doubt that, Lady." She finished the fruit and went to wash her hands.

Annabelle continued her conversation and discussed her

issues so that there would be minimal males at the start of her treatment.

Mel returned from the lav and smiled. "Getting excited to be back in the Imperium?"

Annabelle nodded. "I want to run around on soil. I want not to be afraid all the time. It isn't much, but it's what I want."

"I want that for you, too. I also want you to stop travelling with the circus freak. You deserve a chance to live your life without someone looking behind you and asking questions."

Annabelle sighed. "You aren't a freak. You are just tall. The rest of you is perfectly proportioned. Generously but perfectly. You are taking it too seriously."

"I am stuck in this for life, so I am taking it very seriously."

Annabelle blinked. "They can't undo it?"

"It was always a one-way trip." She sighed. "To be frank, I told the avatar back home that as long as things were over, whether I died up here or died at home, I just wanted things to happen fast. I got my wish."

The specialist blinked. "Right. Did the fruit work?"

"It lifted my mood. I don't feel like jumping out an airlock right now."

"That's good."

"I think so. I also tried something Liona recommended. At least I know where my limbs are at any given time." She smiled.

Ves called out for the meal, and they headed back to the dispenser area. Everyone got their meal, and Mel got her two. Marko was happily eating seeds and cracking nuts, ignoring the raw vegetables that had been prepared.

Mel ate with one hand and held the vegetables for her buddy. When Mel held them, the vegetables were eaten.

Annabelle smiled. "Does she eat noodles?"

"Yes. Noodles are tomorrow's snack."

Annabelle laughed. "How long have you had her?"

"She was with my brother, and when he died fifteen years ago, she came to me. My nephew is out of town, and she scares the hell out of my niece's church group."

Annabelle started laughing. "Oh, yeah, I can see that."

"So, it was either take her with me, or her life would be over."

"Oh, right. How old was she?"

"Close to fifty. This was a second chance for both of us. At least she's having fun."

Mel looked at her buddy, happily cracking nuts and chortling as she swayed from foot to foot.

Two more days to Rai.

Mel sat in an observation area and watched a full wall of stars flow by. She could see the occasional ship, and the kid in her felt like frantically waving like she had when a boat passed under any bridge that she was on.

She sipped a cup of tea and leaned back as they approached the elaborate station.

Ves spoke softly. "Rai is guarded by a security screen, which means we can't come and go as we like. They don't have a Drai guarding the surface."

"Right, so if I blow the customs interview, only Annabelle goes down."

"Not even her. There will have to be appeals and requests."

"Oh, so a lot is riding on me not blowing this."

"Yes. Marko could be with you, but it isn't recommended."

She chuckled and sipped at the tea before saying, "Does she still qualify as a live being?"

"She qualifies as sentient technology."

"Oh, cool. Is she bio-secure?"

"Yes, her feathers don't come out, and the tech handles her waste. She is bio-secure."

"Nice. One less question to deal with."

She nodded. "Is this outfit appropriate?"

"Yes. There are outer robes if you wish to obscure yourself slightly."

"That might be a good idea. I can go in disguised as an obelisk." She chuckled. "I have spent my life not standing out and just doing my job, but now, I have no job, and I stand out just by standing up."

"You sent your measurements to Ageka?"

"I did."

"Good. A day at the retreat might be nice for you."

She paused. "I am not staying, am I?"

"If the retreat allows, you can stay a few days."

"Oh. Right. That won't be uncomfortable at all."

Ves said softly, "It will be fine, Mel. The Rai are very polite."

"Yeah, politeness can disguise a lot of things. Manners can cover a lot of hostility." She asked the room at large, "Why am I out here again?"

"To become a mate of a member of a high-gravity species with specific characteristics."

"Oh, yes. When is that going to kick in?"

He chuckled. "In good time. A match was found suddenly, and there were tasks that had to be completed. Patience, Mel."

"Sure. You are a voice in a station. Patience must be easy for you."

He sighed. "We are getting ready to park. Please get ready to enter the shuttle."

Mel focused on the viewer again and saw the station arms easing up to greet them. "Right. I am going to put on that robe."

She brought her teacup with her and set it in the kitchen before she went and found an open panel in her wall that had a lightweight robe that would cover her suit and still leave her able to defend herself if necessary.

Ves remained near the station, and Mel nodded and straightened, walking past Annabelle's room and confirming it was empty. She headed down to the cargo area, where the shuttle was waiting. Marko flew in and settled on the pad on Mel's shoulder.

"Marko, you aren't supposed to come with me. I have to do customs chit-chat, and you tend to get irritated with the procedure."

"Be good, baby."

"Ves, can I take her along?"

Ves chuckled. "You are responsible for her. Several Rai speak English, and she is fluent in Imperial and Alliance common."

"Oh, yeah. Well, at least it will be interesting."

She nodded. "Any other advice?"

"Remain calm."

"Lovely. So, if they let us go, you will bring us to the surface."

"I am not leaving you, Mel. You will be safe. I would not take you into danger."

She nodded. "Yeah, I am getting that feeling. Well, here we go."

She walked to the shuttle, and Marko hopped to her padded little perch. Annabelle looked at her with a smile. "Here we go."

"Here we go. Excited to be back with regular talents again?"

Annabelle smiled. "A little. I am going to miss you and Marko. You two make an impression."

Mel nodded. "I will miss you, too. Okay, here we go. Ves?"

"I have a berth assigned. Here we go." They lifted and left the larger ship and proceeded to the station.

Time to face customs.

The officers took one look at her and waved her and her

tiny crew off to the side where larger scanning equipment was available.

"Miss, what are the metal implants in your limbs?"

"Supports. I was born to a smaller species, Annabelle's species actually, and because of my growth, reinforcement was necessary."

"I see. What species are you now?"

"Altered Terran, as far as I know. No one has given me a definitive species as I have been altered for three, so I am not sure what the scans are showing."

They nodded. "Well, you are biologically stable, and there is no reason you cannot enter the station. The bot is yours?"

"It is." She didn't explain further.

"Do not let it out of your sight. They are valuable."

"Yes, sir. Thank you."

The man smiled, and she turned her head to see where Annabelle was nearly hopping from foot to foot.

"Can you direct me toward the Nyal Guardian representatives?"

"Oh, they have offices on three. Simply go into this lift and up to the third floor. Turn left, and you will be there."

"Thank you."

She stepped up to Annabelle and smiled. "Third floor.

Come along."

Marko remained quiet, they got into the lift that barely had room for Mel, and they headed up to three.

The transaction was surprisingly straightforward. A scan was administered to Annabelle to confirm that she hadn't aged those sixteen years, and from there, the reward was authorized.

Annabelle looked back. "Mel?"

Mel looked to the men in armoured suits. "Can you send seven hundred fifty thousand to the Citadel on Annabelle's account and give her the two hundred fifty thousand directly?"

The man with blue skin and white eyes smiled. "What about the other million?"

Annabelle blinked. "What?"

"There has been a bump to it."

Mel shrugged. "Put it all in Annabelle's accounts. I don't have any and don't really need anything."

The guardian paused. "You don't have accounts?"

"No. Don't need them. The station provides what I need, and I don't really fit anything in the marketplace."

The guardian blinked. "Oh, right. Well, Specialist, you are now free of obligation to the Citadel, and the funds are in your account."

Mel asked, "Where did the funds appear from?"

"The soon-to-be-empress added them."

"Of course."

Annabelle frowned. "If you get an account, I will transfer that other million to you. I don't need it for anything."

The Guardians were grinning.

Mel chuckled. "Not used to folks trying to share a reward with each other?"

"No. Not used to two women trying to support each other with no thought to themselves."

Annabelle smiled. "Sirs, can you direct us to the visitor's centre? We are authorized to head down to the surface but want to make sure everything is organized."

"I will escort you, ladies. The station can be confusing."

Annabelle checked her wrist unit and exhaled. "And there is the Citadel acknowledgement, and there are the funds."

Mel smiled. "Thank you, Guardian. Just make sure you take us through paths with high ceilings."

He laughed, they walked for five minutes, then they got in line, and someone took their names. There was a startled look at a datapad, and then the male said, "Please come with me."

Mel and Annabelle followed him, and Mel ducked under

the doorway.

They were taken to a quiet room, and tea was provided.

Annabelle asked, "What's going on?"

"Well, Amethyst is married to Lord Akutan, who is the head of Rai. He was a guardian named Blade, and his niece is using the family hero name still. She's Terran from the first wave. Then there is Kyna, who is married to another retired guardian, and she is the Rai recruiter and is starting her family. She is a Terran Reset and lives as a daughter of the house to Ageka, an ex-guardian known as the Sacred Flame. So, Terran's are usually welcome. We come in peace and are useful and respectful."

"They won't expect me to marry anyone?"

"No. You are coming as a wounded warrior. You need time to find yourself again, and that is what the resort is all about. It's a good thing you have the funds. Like any good resort, they are pricey."

"Do you want to stay a few days?" Annabelle asked. "My treat."

"It isn't really in my plans. I am not comfortable around people, and seeing others of my species makes my heart hurt because I don't blend in anymore."

Someone knocked softly on the door, and a man came in,

knelt, and looked at Mel in surprise. "A Vendari. That is surprising. It wasn't on your customs entry."

"You were born a Rai?"

He nodded. "I was."

"What are you now?"

"Um, a Rai?"

"I was born on Terra. Lived as a Terran, and now I am a Terran in Vendari skin."

He looked at her and nodded. "Understood. So, you wish to visit Rai?"

"Yes. Apparently, the Ladies Kyna and Amethyst wish to have tea with us, with Lady Ageka providing security." Mel name-dropped with those she was comfortable with. She had talked to all of the ladies in question.

He turned to Annabelle. "You are staying at the resort?"

"Yes. I require therapy and need to find a new direction for my life. I am not able to commit to a guardian position in my current state, and I will not return to the Citadel."

"Are you looking to immigrate to Rai?"

Annabelle blinked. "No. I want to return to the stars. I am looking for comfort and healing. A place to be safe."

"You aren't safe with your current companions?"

Mel said softly. "I am extremely emotionally unstable, and

my transformation isn't done yet. I am also set up for heavy gravity, and having to keep things light is difficult as it curtails naked day. There isn't a balance with me. My companion and the ship that I am on are very patient, but I need to be able to walk around in a suit that doesn't have to have compression capabilities."

"Really? You should feel so much lighter in normal gravity."

"The suits hold me in and keep my movements small, so I don't go scampering out an airlock."

Annabelle asked, "What?"

"It is like being wrapped in Bungie cords. If I reach out, it pulls me back."

"So, you are under restraints?"

"Kind of like a full-body wrap in elastic."

"I had no idea. You move so easily."

"Yeah, that is just practice."

The interviewer looked at them. "I judge you are no danger to Rai. Your application to take your small shuttle down directly is authorized."

"How long do we have?"

"You have three hours to get to the grid and begin drop procedures. Ms Melora, you have three days maximum on the surface before you leave. Are we understood?"

"Absolutely. Please send the data to my ship."

"Not your com?"

"I don't have one." She shrugged.

"You should get one. They are useful for containing travel documents."

"Well, my skin surface is as dense as an armour plate, so when I find a convenient laser, I will get one installed then."

His eyes widened. "Of course. I hadn't considered... Right, the information is at your shuttle. Please proceed."

Mel asked, "Where do we go?"

"Oh, I will have an assistant take you there." The man in the kimono stood and smiled.

She smiled and set her tea down carefully, standing carefully in full cosplay mode. His eyes lit with appreciation.

She shrugged. "Only way to stand up in loose clothing."

He grinned. "Indeed."

His assistant came in and was directed to bring them back to the berth where their shuttle was waiting.

Annabelle murmured, "Can you show me how to stand up like that?"

"Sure. We have an hour or two." She chuckled.

The assistant nodded. "Have a lovely visit to Rai."

They entered the vessel, and Marko heard something in the distance and perked up. "Come on, Marko, we have to get going."

Marko shrieked and flew down the walkways, a group of Citadel staff turned toward them, and one of them raised a hand to Annabelle.

Mel paused. "We have a few hours if you want to chat with them."

Annabelle shook her head. "I can send a message."

"Eager to get down?"

"Oh, yeah. Have you ever felt that this is what was supposed to happen?"

"I did, and then I woke up blue and nearly nine feet tall. Now I think I might just have needed some ice cream."

Annabelle laughed. They settled in while Ves got his clearances arranged, and then they were on their way through the protective grid in the shield around the gorgeous and protected world of Rai.

Mel talked Annabelle through standing from a kneeling position, and then they were entering the atmosphere, and the world turned to flame outside the shuttle.

CHAPTER SIX

Mel exited with Marko on her shoulder and walked toward the Rai Guardians, who had come to them to make sure that they were legitimate.

"Pardon me, sirs and madams, which way to the retreat?"

The Guardians grinned, and one woman asked, "Are you really the same species as Kyna?"

"Yeah, though no one will confuse me for a snow bunny."

They laughed, and with the ice broken, they led them down a path that ended in a lovely little set of buildings with private bathing areas and a wide outer structure that faced an inner courtyard. The sliding doors were beautiful.

Annabelle whispered, "What are you thinking?"

"I am thinking that the Admaryn and Yokai got along really well."

"What are Yokai?"

"Japanese elves and fairies and the mix."

"No way."

"Way. You know that the Admaryn tried to kill humanity, right?"

"Uh, no."

"Well, they knocked us back down to almost nothing in quite a few regions."

Annabelle blinked. "How do you know all this stuff?"

"History was played into my brain during my delivery flight."

A group of women in kimonos walked toward them, and Mel smiled and bowed thirty degrees.

Ageka paused and laughed. "Of course, that is all we would get from a Vedari."

"That is all you get from a Terran who can't quite get a grip on her own body. Still growing."

"Fair enough. So, what would you like to do first? Get changed?"

Mel smiled. "This is Annabelle; she is here to go through therapies. I am merely here dropping her off and to have a chat with Amethyst and Kyna."

"Yes, they told me. I thought you would like to be properly

attired."

"I don't think you have my size, and I don't have the means to pay for anything."

"We have put something together for you. Can you sit or kneel or something?" Ageka muttered.

"Not in the dirt."

The woman blinked, and she realized what she had been saying. "Right. Annabelle, please go with these ladies, and they will check you in. Melora, please come with me."

Mel looked at Annabelle. The smaller woman hugged her. "I want to see you before you leave, Mel. You, too, Marko."

Marko chittered and bobbed affirmative.

Annabell let Mel go, smiled, and left with the other ladies.

Ageka nodded. "Come with me, Melora."

"Sure, Ageka."

They walked down the lane to a teahouse, and there were a few ladies there with folded fabric.

"Lady Amethyst has offered you a memory of Rai. Please kneel at the edge of the deck."

Mel nodded and knelt. They eased off her robe, and Ageka asked, "Why do you need the suit?"

"It controls my limbs and keeps me from flying in lower gravity, apparently. Like a leash on an animal."

Ageka blinked. "Oh, right. We will leave it on."

"Thought you might."

She was directed to put her arms out, and three layers were yanked and tucked around her. One woman muttered about a waste of fabric in Rai.

Mel sighed and responded, "*Yes, I understand. I am not to grips with it myself.*"

The woman flushed and bowed in apology. "I meant no offense, lady."

"Yes, you did. You just didn't think I would understand. Are we done?"

Ageka said, "One more layer."

When Mel was wearing three layers of smoothed robes, a sash was wrapped around her waist, and it snugged everything together. There was no way to get the Obi into standard configuration.

"Thank you, ladies."

She got up, and Ageka blinked. "Did you grow since you sent the information?"

"Yes. I told you that."

"I didn't expect it to be this much."

"Sorry. I can remove this, and you can recycle it into a wardrobe for all the staff."

Ageka laughed and said, "Come with me."

Mel walked carefully and tried to balance her weight as she let Ageka get ahead of her.

The ladies were looking cute and sitting under a silk canopy that had obviously been set up for her. Mel walked up silently and bowed. "Ladies."

Amethyst got up, her black hair pinned high on her head. Kyna's crimson hair was half up, half down. She got up and smiled. "You are a Reset?"

"Apparently."

"To what?"

"Something called a Vendari."

Kyna looked around. "Where is he?"

"I don't know. I have been on my own since I woke up. Well, until Annabelle floated past."

Marko squawked and thudded to her shoulder. "And Marko. Marko has been with me, but she's on good behaviour here."

Kyna blinked. "Is that a parrot?"

"She was. Nearly at her expiry date when I got the offer, so she had to come with me. She jokes she gave me her feathers."

Kyna chuckled and nodded to Marko. "Greetings, Marko, welcome to Rai."

Marko flapped happily and stuck out her beak for pets. Mel lifted her hand, and her buddy stepped onto her wrist. She lowered the bird to where Kyna could give her scratchies.

"I thought it would feel like metal, but it's so soft, like feathers."

Marko was on good behaviour and chortled happily.

Amethyst joined in, and eventually, Marko was back on Mel's shoulder, and they were all sitting down for a meal.

Mel looked at the foods. "I am just going to use my fingers if that is acceptable."

Kyna nodded. "It is very acceptable. The bowls are coming now."

Mel carefully washed her hands and dried her fingertips.

The food was good, a little awkward, but it was shared with ladies who felt the distance from home, and it felt nice to be there with them.

Mel looked at Kyna. "Can you help Annabelle find her path? She feels very lost, with patches of panic when she thinks I am not paying attention. I have seen that before, and she's going to pretend to be normal until she blows."

Mel sipped at the small food bowl that was doubling for her teacup. "She may feel better when she learns that some of those men have been Darwined."

Amethyst and Kyna chuckled. Kyna said, "Well, you are looking for a hobby."

"Yeah, but I am dependent on Ves to get around." She tapped her lips with a finger. "I do have access to all the information attached to the pod she was in. I should be able to figure something out from there. My problem is stealth. That is one thing I don't have."

Kyna nodded. "Right."

"Look at me, bitch!" Marko raised her wings.

"You aren't stealthy either, twit. You are a giant cursing, silver bird."

Marko looked sly and moved coquettishly. *"Pretty bird."*

"Yes, honey, you are a very pretty bird."

Marko started grooming her hair.

"Weirdo."

There was more chortling as the hair was straightened strand by strand.

She swayed as the grooming relaxed her.

If you are tired, you can come and rest on board the shuttle, Mel. Ves's voice was soft in her mind.

Kyna blinked. "What was that?"

"Ves was talking to me. He offered me a nap spot."

"Ves is the avatar?"

Mel kept her lids low. "No, Ves is the Vendari Station computer."

Kyna paused. "Oh. Oh dear. Has the computer been really attentive to you? Consoling you?"

Mel heard the suspicion. "Yes."

"Station computers don't have nurturing personalities. They have cold and efficient personalities. Whatever Ves is, he isn't a standard computer."

"Yeah. I know. I have known for a while."

You have?

"Ves, I was delivered to the station. That means that my caretaker was supposed to be there. Since he was the only one there, it had to be him."

Ah, yeah. I hadn't noticed you noticing that.

She smiled and stroked Marko's side. "I think I should say goodbye to Annabelle and get my butt back in the shuttle."

Kyna smiled. "You have an emotional attachment to the computer."

"He looked up how to deal with PMS in a giant human. That is some niche research. I have a ton of fruit from Veth that has a lovely mood-boosting effect when I am feeling blue." She smiled. "I think he is freeze-drying it to add to my morning tea."

Amethyst laughed. "That's a great feature."

"Yeah, I am going to tell Liona about the powdered stuff. I had a friend who was a prepper and freeze-dried everything. It's a nice way to sneak vegetables into everything." Mel smiled. "Thanks for the meal and the conversation."

Kyna said, "Do you want to stay overnight?"

"I would love to say yes, but crawling into a room where a bunch of beds have been shoved together to fit me doesn't sound appealing."

Kyna wrinkled her nose. "Right. I see what would happen there."

"Plus, I need a blanket and a pillow. I am a fussy sleeper."

Amethyst nodded. "Gotcha."

Mel moved to her feet, and Kyna chuckled. "I wish I was that graceful."

"When you grow up, you can be just like me." Mel grinned.

She picked up the folded robe and looked at Amy. "Where do you want the kimono?"

"Keep it. It is our gift to you."

"I am going to outgrow it even more in a few days. I am serious. It will be too small for me, and Marko doesn't wear robes."

She tugged at the sash, and the robe easily opened as if it

was under strain. She slid the layers off her shoulders and folded the fabric over her arm.

"It has been lovely meeting you, ladies. Thank you for being so hospitable."

Kyna smiled. "It was our pleasure."

Amethyst smiled. "Come back for a visit whenever you like."

"When things have settled and I can learn who I am again." She gestured. "Or learn who this is. There is one thing: people are very nice to me. If that is a side effect I can control, I want to."

"You don't want people to be nice to you?"

"If it is a side effect of the Vendari genes, I want to control it. This is probably why they got in trouble to begin with."

She shrugged. "There had to be a reason that other populations tried to stamp them out and succeeded."

Amethyst blinked. "That would definitely make you feel some instability."

"Yeah. All my life I have fought to keep my head above water, fought to make a place for myself in the world, but now, I wouldn't even know where to start." She shrugged. "Just when I feel I have gotten the hang of it, I grow again, have to balance again, and when I stumble, I hit the walls.

Marko tried to catch me once, but she got a bit squished. So now, she just encourages me. I play lots of basketball back at the station."

Kyna asked, "Where are you going next?"

"Possitt II. Yet another pregnant reset." She smiled. "You look cute, Kyna."

Kyna blushed. "How did you know? I am not showing."

"You have two heartbeats but only one Terran heart, and a mid-belly beat isn't a standard adaptation." She smiled. "Liona is pregnant as well, but hers is going to take longer."

Kyna was blushing. "Interesting talent."

"I have always known when folks were pregnant, but now, I can hear it." She slipped her robe on and carried the folded kimono and sash. "So, where am I going? I need to say goodbye to Annabelle."

Ageka smiled and then scowled as she saw the fabric in Mel's grip. "Are our offerings not sufficient for you?"

"Lady Ageka, you are forgetting that I am still growing. This will be knee-high by the end of the week. That isn't a good look, and you can use the fabric to clothe others, guests, anyone you like. It was pleasant to wear it, but as I am not finished yet, it would just take up space with clothing I cannot use. I am living at the grace of the Vendari Station and cannot fill space that isn't mine."

Ageka blinked, and understanding filled her gaze. "I believe I understand."

"So, please, allow me to return this with my thanks for allowing me to wear it during my visit."

Ageka sighed and accepted the folds. "Thank you for folding it properly."

"You are welcome. It was very pretty, but I think it clashed with my hair or hands."

The older woman laughed.

"May I say goodbye to Annabelle? I promised I would."

"Of course. Please come with me. She is comfortable, fed, and in the meditation garden."

"Good. I will be quick."

She nodded to her lunch companions and said, "I will be right back."

She walked with Ageka to the meditation garden where Annabelle was kneeling on a cushion on a wide, flat stone.

Marko launched and landed near Annabelle, squawking softly. The specialist opened her eyes and looked around. "Oh, are you going so soon?"

Mel stood waiting, and when Annabelle got up and walked over to her, she smiled at the hug. "Hey, you rest, get better, and find out what you want to do."

"I will. You take care of yourself, and be kind to yourself." Annabelle mumbled into her chest. "Let Ves take care of you, too. And eat the fucking fruit. Your PMS is terrifying."

Mel laughed. "It always was. It's where Marko learned half of her cursing."

The hug got tighter, and she looked up at her. "I am going to set something up for your return to the orbital station."

"I will be there in a few hours."

"I can make a fast call. I think I know what you need to complete the outfit. Something to give it some pizzaz."

"Wait. Clothing?"

"This will fit. Trust me. You are going to have to stare down a l'nal, though."

"Oh. Big spider?"

"Very big. Your height, actually."

"Fun."

"I will get Fade to help me with the contact or maybe Ageka."

"If you like. Tell them to leave a message for Ves. He will let me know."

Annabelle smiled. "Thanks for being a friendly face at a distance when I came out."

"Thanks for not freaking out when I stood up."

"Thanks for being a friend, even if you were a bit morose sometimes. You have cause."

"Call Ves whenever you want to talk to me."

Annabelle smiled. "I will. I have all the contact information."

Mel smiled. "You need to let go now."

Annabelle chuckled. "You caught that."

"I did. You are safe; they will take care of you and help you to take care of yourself. If you find a guy, remember that they frown on premarital sex here."

Annabelle looked at her in shock. "I wouldn't..."

"Never say never. Now, do what you need to do. I need to head back to Ves."

Marko hopped over, and Annabelle whispered her goodbye when Marko replied, *"Fuck off, bitch!"*

"Right. Love you, too, Marko."

Marko returned to Mel's shoulder, and they began to walk cautiously through the retreat. Amethyst and Kyna came with them and walked them to the ship.

There were hugs, there were well wishes, and then Mel and Marko were in a slowly rising shuttle, heading back to the station to have themselves frisked and the shuttle examined for any contraband.

"Mel, there is a seamstress on six waiting for you. Annabelle wasn't lying; she called ahead."

"Is it okay for me to go?"

"It is. No problem. Go ahead." Ves's voice was calm.

She nodded and headed out with her companion while Marko was tense and vibrating as they moved through the station.

Marko flew off when Mel faced the seamstress and started laughing at what had been chosen for her. Hip scarves that would flutter in the breeze when she moved were made available in a lovely array of colours.

Two dress outfits were available, and they were both in a handkerchief style that exposed a lot of her skin but still looked lovely.

"Annabelle went overboard." Mel turned from the left to the right to see herself.

The seamstress and weaver clacked her mandibles. "You are lucky in your friends."

"It is a small collection, but yes, I am."

"Lady Ageka has commissioned a kimono for you when you have completed your growth. Do you know when that will be?"

You have four more inches until you are done.

"I have four more inches until my growth is complete."

"That is acceptable. I can work with that. Where will the work be sent?"

"Um, Vendari Station, I suppose?"

"Ah, you are heavy grav. That explains your restraint system."

Mel smiled. "I guess it does. This is complete?"

"Yes. Change out of things and take the parcel. You can return to your ship feeling much more stylish."

"Thank you, Madame K'vekna."

"You are welcome, Vendari-bride."

Mel blinked but removed the dress, which was folded and tucked in with the scarves. She carried the bundle back to Ves, and Marko flew into the ship just as she stepped onboard. "Okay, Ves. We are ready to travel." She tucked her parcel in her quarters and returned to the seats.

"Very well. Clearance is achieved, and we are on our way back to our warship."

"Wait. Warship?"

"I would never take you out without defenses, Mel. You are precious."

She smiled. "Just fly the ship, Ves."

There was a chuckle, and they glided carefully through traffic and rejoined their larger ship.

Marko was settled in her little three-quarter egg and was chortling happily.

Mel looked at the egg but could only see her buddy preening.

She shrugged and stretched. "I guess it is back to the gym for me."

Ves said softly, "May I speak to you for a moment?"

"Sure. Where do you want to talk?"

"In the dining room."

"Okay. On my way."

Mel headed up to the dining area, and a bot brought her a cup of tea.

"What did you want to talk about, Ves?"

"I believe it is time to show you what I look like and explain why we are here."

"Well, I am all in favour of any information."

A bot moved forward, a projection appeared in front of her, and Mel blinked. "Well, that explains a bit."

He had a red body, blue hair, and green arms. She could tell because he wasn't wearing anything.

She cleared her throat finally. "Did you mean to appear naked?"

The figure smiled, and clothing appeared. Loose silky trousers and a long vest, both white and embroidered with teeny star systems. His ears were pierced in a number of places, and his hair was in a thick braid draped over his shoulder.

"Better?"

"Less distracting and very pretty. So, this is you, Ves?"

"It was. I was attacked during the fall of the Vedari, and that is when Vendar bonded with me. He split me into two beings. One was a blank body that he could use to do maintenance on his worlds, and he left me at the high-security station in stasis, as there was no reason to fix me. He had the body he wanted."

"Oh. Well, you are fixed now."

"Vendar heard about the project and sent the specifications needed for one of our kind. Far sooner than he had imagined, he received notification that you existed, and the transformation could begin. Vendar authorized it, ordered the very long delivery, and flew out in the clone to create a world for you, scavenging ancient buildings and making them new so you would be happy with the world around you."

"What happened to you?"

"He began the repair and recovery process, but I remained in a capsule until I was complete."

"So, you are also the avatar of Vendar?"

"Yes, but as long as he has the clone, there is only a tenuous link between us. He does not need to be actively in control."

"I see. So, why are you speaking about this now?"

"Because I am waking and would like you with me."

"I thought I had to go to Possitt II."

His projection sighed. "You don't have to, but your other Reset member is there."

"I don't really need to meet in person, I don't think. I feel more at home in the station than I do in any court." She shrugged. "You are driving."

He chuckled.

"Oh, your name isn't Ves then?"

"My name was Occorin."

"What is it now? New life, new starts."

"Occor?" He looked at her with a slight smile.

"Occor it is. I will probably call you Ves when I can't see you."

"That is fair." He paused. "What does Marko have?"

"What? Nothing. She shouldn't have anything with her." She got up. "Is she still in the shuttle?"

"Yes."

"Why are you asking?"

"There has just been a warrant issued for your arrest. Marko took something."

"Shit." She got up and said, "Sorry to leave this discussion. Is that outfit standard wear?"

He chuckled. "It is formal-casual. We don't really wear tight clothing. Everything is light. I am checking to see if the stolen item can be purchased."

"Please tell me you bounced the signal off a few satellites and other ships."

"Of course. They say that they are priceless and a protected species."

"Fuck." Mel ran through the halls to the shuttle and found Marko still in her little pod, making happy crooning noises.

"Marko!"

There was a trill as she lifted her head and looked at Mel.

"What do you have there?"

"Mine, bitch! Hands off, cunt!"

She sighed at the frantic tone. "Honey, let me see who you have there."

Marko looked at her and moved aside. Mel saw the cutest, fluffiest little creatures with wide eyes and stubby little beaks. "Oh, hello, babies. What are you?"

Little, happy, warm images flowed into Mel's mind as the tiny creatures hopped excitedly.

Ves spoke softly. "I have some data on them. They are called Yaluthu and are an emotional symbiote for those they feel a connection to. The Citadel controls them, and I am getting this information from Annabelle."

"Wise choice. Oh, they are hungry."

Ves paused. "What?"

"They are hungry. Marko, can I take them, and Ves will help get something to eat?"

Ves murmured, "What do they need?"

"Finely crushed high-protein seeds. Marko can do the crushing if you get the larger seeds ready."

"Right. They are on their way."

Mel looked at Marko. "You go to the food dispenser and start making food for the babies, okay? I will carry them."

Marko looked and huffed with uncertainty.

Mel just scooped up the Yaluthu and started walking. The little ones were chirping happily, and a hungry note came into their voices. That got Marko's attention. She shot past Mel, screaming epithets for her to follow.

Mel grinned and followed with the little creatures wiggling against her hands and chirping encouragement.

Marko had made a large pile of dust on the table, and Mel let the little ones hop out of her hands and over to the food. She went and got a shallow dish of water and brought it out for them, setting it a few inches away from the food.

Mel smiled as she watched the little ones going at it under the watchful eye of Marko.

One of the little ones was crimson and gold, and the other was silver and vivid blue. The fluff around their eyes started the wave of stripes that covered their bodies.

"They are cute, Marko. I can see the attraction."

Marko watched over them and kept nudging them to the food. She was crooning a special song for them, and it made Mel smile. "You're a good mom, Marko. You swear a lot but still a good mom."

Marko chortled and watched the little ones eat.

Mel smiled. "I have to go and see if I can do damage control." She scratched under Marko's chin, and the crimson Yaluthu stopped eating. When she took a few steps away, the little one flapped after her, cheeping loudly.

Marko screeched. "*Up!*"

"Shit. Right. Up. First, drink some water, baby, and then I will just take you with me."

The little red buddy just turned around and hopped with a funny left-to-right motion, drank, and then turned back to her with the out-of-control frenzy of a windup toy.

"Oh, wow. Okay. Do you want to be carried or..."

Marko squawked. *"Up, up."*

"Right. Up, up." Mel carefully scooped up the tiny creature and frowned, shrugged, and put it on her left shoulder. The bursts of cheerful delight that rocked through her were infectious. She smiled as the stresses of the last few months seemed to wash away.

"Uh-oh." She sighed and stroked the tiny creature with a fingertip. "Did she steal you for me?"

There was the sound of Marko shrieking when they arrived at the station and, then, while Mel was entering the seamstress's shop, the sight of Marko and her landing near them. The two ran to their new mama the moment that Mel whistled. The beings around the Yaluthu realized that they were being taken by the bird when they were halfway to the shuttle. There was shouting behind them, but Marko was already inside the closed shuttle, and they were on their way to their ship.

Mel winced. "Oh. So, they are pissed."

The little fluffy thing purred and rubbed against her neck. It didn't care. It had found its person.

"Uh-oh." Mel sighed and went to deal with the fallout of being bonded by a creature smaller than her hand.

CHAPTER SEVEN

Mel sat in her chair and tossed a basketball in the air as the official from the Citadel reamed her out.

"*Yaluthu are treasured beings, and they are needed for those who have suffered trauma. To have you simply abduct them as pets is sheer piracy.*"

"I didn't abduct them." She kept tossing the ball, and her little friend remained on her shoulder.

"*Abduct, stole. I don't know what you think you will gain by it, but they are not to be disposed of so lightly.*"

"I didn't abduct them. My companion spoke to them and explained our situation, and then two little ones volunteered to be with us. My companion just brought them to the ship. Now, they are sharing emotions and conversing with us."

She balanced the ball on her fingertip and ignored the

angry green man in Citadel robes. "Sir, do you have anyone there with a Yaluthu that can speak to this situation?"

"There is one, but they are in pursuit of your vessel."

"Fun. I hope they like high gravity."

"You have the Yaluthu in high gravity?" He was horrified.

The enthusiastic cheeping made her grin. "It doesn't seem to mind."

"What is its name?"

She chuckled. "Whee."

"What?"

"Whee. It thinks of me and says *Whee*, so it is Whee."

She stood so the little creature was visible, and it slid down her arm saying, "Whee," before it chirped happily and climbed up her again.

The little red and gold menace was relentless as it climbed up her arm. Beak and pudgy claws, it made it back to her shoulder.

The Citadel staffer was astonished. *"You have still stolen it."*

"Great. The great Yaluthu piracy. Give me the information of the representative chasing me, and I will get in touch with them."

"Why?"

"Because if they want to chase me down, I want them to

take the most efficient route." Mel grinned.

He paused and gave her the call sign. *"All Alliance and Imperium vessels are looking for you."*

"Okay. I am fine with that."

She got the information, and Ves got to work on it. She waved farewell and ended the call.

Ves said, "They were not kidding. The removal of the Yaluthu from a space station has given you and Marko a pirate classification."

"Well, that has to be a very interesting thing. I am surprised it was so easy to break the law. All I had to do was pick up some shopping."

"Indeed. Oh, we can install a com now. Your body is finished growing."

"Now?"

"Yes. Now. You completed the last surge after you arrived on the shuttle. Don't you feel it?"

She flexed her hands and felt that the pain that had been in her body, the pervasive ache that had worn on her mood and her thoughts, was finally over.

Whee chirped happily.

"The files I can gain on the Yaluthu indicate that they are empathetic healers who bond and then assist their companion as the Yaluthu continues to their mature state."

"What is their mature state?"

"Something similar to Marko."

"Ohh. That would be why she thought they were her babies, though she did give Whee up easily."

"Marko has carried her youngling into your quarters and is teaching it to grip a stand. It is doing very well."

"I think we are going to make a united front. Marko! Bring the baby."

Marko flew in a moment later with her little one clinging to her leg sideways. Mel bit her lip to stop her laugh as Marko landed on her right shoulder, and the little one snuggled in next to her. Well, they were as ready as they were going to be.

Ves sighed. "I am making the connections through as many relay stations as I can. They are serious. They are furious."

"Right. Start the call."

A human face with a raptor on her shoulder was glaring at her. *"Who are you, and why did you steal Rumble's babies?"* The woman frowned. *"And why are they a different colour now?"*

"Is Rumble your Yaluthu?"

"Yes. Those are his fluffles."

"My bird, Marko, brought them to the shuttle. I must say, since Whee has been with me, I feel better than I did since leaving Earth."

The woman stared. *"Earth?"*

"Yes. I am a reset Terran. It's part of a project run by our avatar and the Nyal Imperium. I have been set for heavy gravity and have been feeling very isolated."

The woman's fury faded. *"You called it Whee?"*

"It climbs me and slides down my arm. Marko's little one is Pohloh."

The woman smiled. *"I see. Got it. Well, my name is Addy, and I am normally in charge of Citadel Iratho. I was out to Rai to pick up a staff member, but she is down on the surface."*

Mel smiled. "Annabelle. She's getting some therapy she desperately needs. She wasn't going to be able to face the bill the Citadel was going to give her for looking for her while she was in stasis after her torture."

Addy smiled politely. *"What?"*

"We were notified that her Citadel wasn't going to take her back without plenty of money, so we collected the reward for her safe return, and then, she got it, paid her bill, and headed down to Rai to figure out what she wants."

Whee nuzzled her cheek and chirped in her ear.

Addy paused. *"I am going to get to the bottom of that, but how tall are you?"*

"Around nine feet. We have one more stop before I get to find out if my proposed partner is awake."

"What?"

"It's a heavy-grav thing. So, they have already bonded to me and Marko, so I don't know what we are supposed to do now."

"Oh, right. They only bond if you are suitable and you have a need, and then their lifespan matches yours. What is your lifespan?"

"No clue."

"Well, when you are stable, they are going to start eating a ton, then they moult, and after that, the fluffles show up. Each clutch is different, but they are self-propagating and don't become pretty raptors like this until they have littles."

"That is helpful. What do they eat? Marko is grinding up seeds and stuff for them."

"Uh, when they start packing on the weight, they want shredded meat. Ration packs are fine." Addy smiled. *"When they told me a giant blue alien had my Yaluthu, I confess, I wanted to blast you out of the sky."*

"Well, I am glad you didn't. Vendar would be upset that he has been nosey and tried to get me into his space."

The human's eyes flashed, and the voice was different. *"Beloved of Vendar, it is good you are here. His solitude has not been* good for him. Even our kind suffers from lack of social interaction. Vendar has always been with his people. When he lost them, it hurt him."

Addy's eyes flickered. *"Well, that was Iratho. He rarely takes over."* She sighed. *"Rumble wants to see his offspring. Can we meet at a neutral site?"*

Mel paused. "Ves?"

"We will continue on to our destination. I will send them arrival information, and the proof of life can be held there."

"Okay."

Addy smiled. *"Got it. We will meet you there."*

The call disconnected, and Whee nuzzled her, chirping in concern. Pohloh and Marko preened each other happily. The concern wasn't shared.

"They are making plans to arrest you upon your landing on Possitt II."

"Oh. Well, that sucks. She seemed so nice."

"Adelheid is a world breaker."

"What?"

"She creates a concussive blast that can crack worlds."

"Oh. So, that would hurt."

"You would survive it, but it would ache a bit." Ves sighed. "Agree to their terms, and I will sort it with Iratho."

"Are you doing that right now?"

"I am. His female avatar is being told that her Yaluthu is upset and worried for his children. She is acting on that worry."

"I can understand that. I feel that way about Marko." She reached up and stroked her big buddy.

She leaned back. "So, what am I wearing to Possitt II?"

Ves laughed. "One of the dresses that you got at the station would be appropriate, as would one of the suits I made you."

She smiled. "I am going to compromise. How long until we arrive?"

"Three days. Plenty of time for you to get familiar with your new additions. The dispensers have been altered so that the Yaluthu can get themselves food if hungry."

"I am going to keep plenty of it around the ship. If they grow like I did, food is what will build them up." She smiled. "It will also give them endorphins to help them ignore the pain."

Ves asked. "You were in pain?"

"Oh, yes. My bones ached. Every muscle, every tendon. It all hurt. I was nearly doubled in size, and I am three or four times my standard Terran weight."

She shrugged. "It hurts because growing hurts, and I am

going to try and ease it for the Yaluthu." She stroked Whee. "Right, Whee?"

Whee chirped excitedly, and Mel got up with the entire menagerie and headed back to the dining area.

She put her arm down, and Whee slid down with her signature sound. Pohloh jumped, and Marko was behind her, ushering her along.

Mel got food out for the littles, and Marko ground it up for both of them until they were sitting in front of enormous piles of crushed grain.

Mel sat with them and stroked Whee as Marko encouraged Pohloh.

When the Yaluthu had finished their enormous meals, Marko brought out a round nut and nudged it with her beak. Soccer began on the table, and the Yaluthu were fun to watch.

The days flew by, and then, the much larger Yaluthu were on her shoulders, with Marko protectively wrapping a wing around Pohloh.

They stood on the ramp of the shuttle and walked out to Possitt II, and Mel stood straight as she faced the gathered crowd of angry Citadel personnel.

She laughed at the man approaching her with heavy cuffs.

"Melora of Terra, you are under arrest for the abduction and diversion of two Yaluthu."

She grinned and extended her hands. He blinked and snapped the cuffs on her wrists. They barely fit. Chains dangled from them, and there was the hum of energy.

"Aw, is that supposed to keep me cuffed? How adorable."

Two of the Citadel members flanked her and tried to grab the Yaluthu. "I would not recommend that."

Whee was vibrating with fury, as was Marko and Pohloh.

"So, where is my trial to be held?"

The Citadel staffers looked at each other.

"Well, you have made accusations and are claiming ownership of the free symbiotic beings that Yaluthu are known to be. They are protected by the Citadel, not controlled, and definitely not owned. They choose their partners, and these two little maniacs have chosen."

Addy walked forward next to another Terran woman in Possitt formal wear. The raptor on her shoulder looked at Whee and Pohloh and then began to shriek happily.

Addy's expression was stunned. "You are kidding."

Her buddy chirped and chortled happily then flew over to Mel and rubbed up against his offspring, and Whee chattered angrily, muttering. It flew around and talked to Pohloh, and the little one and Marko chewed him out.

Addy blushed. "I am so sorry, Mel. Let me get those cuffs."

Mel shrugged and just brushed the cuffs off. "Bondage isn't my thing."

Addy stared. "You weren't cuffed."

"Yes, I was. Until I didn't want to be. Molecular density is a fun toy."

The Possitt Terran came forward. "Melora, I am so sorry about this. Ves contacted me because he thought you would like to meet with another Reset."

"Yes, I can see how well that is working out for me. Rumble, go back to Addy. She needs you now because she can feel the fuck-up washing over her."

Addy blushed. "I..."

"Didn't believe I was human? Didn't believe that I was in pain? You don't have sole ownership of agony. The Yaluthu go where they can do the most good, to the people who need them. Rumble says that he fought your niece and was mad at her for being close but not right, so he knew. Why did you believe his judgment and not that of the littles?"

Whee made a noise that sounded like a raspberry.

Addy blinked. "I didn't know they could make that sound."

Mel smiled. "They are learning from a freaking parrot. They are going to be talking in a few days. They are already three times as heavy. These babies are prepping for heavy gravity. Their offspring will be heavy gravity Yaluthu."

The woman wearing the dress and the circlet said, "Hiya, Mel, I am Amber. I set up tea before the Citadel asked to greet you when you landed."

Addy stood, and her eyes flickered wildly. "Oh shit."

Mel walked toward Amber, and Addy was in the way.

Addy looked at her. "I could destroy you and this world."

"And I can smash you flat. My bones don't turn to jelly, and I don't pull punches. Step aside. I take up a lot of room."

Addy stared and blushed and then winced as Rumble returned to her and began to shriek in her ear.

Amber smiled. "This way. We have set out a lunch."

Mel chuckled. "Music to my ears."

Amber chuckled and led her way through a paved street where traffic had been stopped. Folk were staring at her, but they were smiling, which was a nice change.

Amber said, "That's a nice outfit and lovely sash."

"Thank you. A friend bought me the sash on Rai Station."

They walked to a lovely palace, but Amber walked her around the main structure and out back to a wide stone patio with a very large bistro set. Mel grinned. "Aw, you shouldn't have."

"I thought it would be nice for you to be comfortable."

"I really appreciate that. It has been a rough few months."

"What advice did Imbolt give you?"

"None. I haven't met him. He was on a delivery run while they started processing me. I got launched into space while still growing with Marko here, and from there, I was at a base and trying to keep my balance while I kept getting bigger."

Amber looked at her in shock. "You had to do all of that on your own?"

"Well, I had Marko, but yes, that was the reason that the Yaluthu came. They heard our pain. How did the Citadel reps all get here?"

"They are trying to set up a Citadel on Possitt II. Given their behaviour today, we aren't going to allow that. This behaviour was unhinged, and with a very talented population, we believe in decorum and that does not involve attempting to arrest a guest before they are greeted."

Someone served a large teacup to Mel and a smaller version to Amber. Amber poured for both of them. "You actually were thinking of smashing Addy into the floor?"

"If she attacked me, yes. Nothing unprovoked."

"I must say, I thought you would be leaping over tall buildings."

"Ves figured out I may get a little over-enthused, and this outfit has what is basically a set of resistance bands in it. If I move too freely, it pulls back. It also stops me from being faster than a locomotive."

Amber grinned that she had caught the reference. "Wow. That confirmed it."

"I know, I don't look Terran."

"Your features are, but your body says *smash*."

Mel giggled, and Whee and Marko chuckled. "It feels that way sometimes, but I just want things to get to my new normal."

"You aren't there yet?"

"I have only had Whee for a few days. I am feeling better; I have stopped growing. Now I can find out what this body can do, but Ves continues to taunt me with images of him. Physical him is back on the station, and a different version is out making me a home on one of Vendar's worlds." She grinned. "Apparently, I was a surprise."

Amber smiled. "Just as I was for my husband. Well, less of a surprise and more of a custom modification that came with extras."

"When are you due?"

"Two more months."

"Your husband isn't here?"

She grinned. "No, he's at the Imperial court for the day. I won't catch hell until he hears about you and the Citadel."

"Why?"

"All of their combat specialists were ready to attack you. It wasn't a great place for a preggo lady."

Mel sighed. "No, and I am sorry you were in that position."

"You have always been in the way."

She didn't take offense. "Yes. My mother died, and my father was a bastard until he died, and he taught my brother to be the same way. When he died, he left me his children and a swearing parrot. I got the kids through school but couldn't do much for Marko, so I brought her with me."

Marko lifted her head. *"Pretty girl. Lovely bitch."*

Mel smiled and sipped her tea and ate her sandwich. "The food is nice."

"Thank you. You are fairly near to our system. I would love another visit. I would offer to do it, but my husband is attached to this system."

"I understand. Just issue an invitation, and I can do some travelling. I don't mind it. I have a personal pilot and good friends."

Amber chuckled. "Your shoulder-bound companions?"

"Yeah. They are great, and I feel so much better." She was feeling relaxed. "Can Marko go for a flight? We haven't been in the atmosphere much. She's self-contained, so no worry about bio-contaminants."

"Oh, certainly."

Marko launched herself skyward, and Pohloh snuggled in and rubbed against Mel's head. "One day, you will fly with Marko. You, too, Whee."

The Yaluthu cuddled up next to her.

Amber smiled. "They both are affectionate toward you."

"We all play together, interact together, and work as a group."

"Any sign of your mate?"

"Yes, he's holograming himself into public areas of the ship. We are chatting, and I am learning about him. It could just be an AI, but it's company."

I am not an AI, Melora. AIs can't communicate on the psychic plain.

Mel smiled. "He didn't like me saying that."

Amber blinked. "He's listening?"

"Yes, I have filaments for tracking and communication as

well as biofeedback in my brain. He put them in himself."

"Ouch."

"Yeah, well, they were necessary to control my growth and get my body to alter pigment. The Vendari were the third species I was prepped for because the first two had easier growth stages."

"Wow. So, what did you do back home?"

"Bits of anything. Waited tables, drove an ambulance, drove an ambulance in combat, back to waiting tables, and finally retired to my hometown and helped my brother's family after his death. The cancer kind of took my career plans and trashed them. The fumbling of my transformation to giant kind of suits my track record. The attempted arrest was new."

"Addy was upset because she wanted to keep the babies. She thought that there was no way they would take off on their own, so kidnapping was the only thing that sprang to mind, and she has a thick mama-bear streak."

"I get it. I don't blame her."

"May I ask her to join us? She doesn't get off Iratho frequently. She wanted to do something nice for her Yaluthu, but intent and execution often fumble." Amber raised a hand, and a servant appeared out of nowhere. They nodded and scuttled away.

"I guessed you would say yes. Now, we will see what the secondary avatar says. She just woke up after years of being stored because of the danger of her talent. They let her go on Iratho after an entire island had been prepared for her so she wouldn't break the world. She learned to control herself, and then she got her Yaluthu and calmed right down." Amber sipped at her tea. "Now we see if she can flush her embarrassment and make a friend."

Mel looked up and watched Marko soaring happily.

A few minutes later, Addy walked in with the servant, and a chair was set for her at the table with a full set of implements and a service.

Addy sighed, and Rumble hopped off her shoulder, ran up to Mel, and flapped his wings. Mel put her hand on the table, and he ran up her arm to preen Whee. She reached up and moved Pohloh to the other side.

Addy blinked. "What were you doing on Rai Station?"

"Oh, I was on Rai dropping off a Citadel specialist that washed up outside my station. We brought her in and talked to her, talked to her Citadel, and they told us that for her to get any help, she needed a quarter of a million credits to pay off the search and rescue efforts from when she was stolen."

Mel smiled as she listened to the family reunion on her shoulder. Whee was already bigger than her progenitor by a few inches. They changed to match their others.

Mel continued, "So, we contacted the Imperium, and they said there was a million-credit reward for any lost Terrans, so we made arrangements and handed her over to the Guardians, who paid the Citadel. Then, we took her down to Rai so she could get some therapy for the multiple sexual assaults and find the things that light her soul, which is what Kyna is good at. So, she will be retrained as a guardsman if she chooses to be and will get the help she needs to stop screaming in her sleep."

Addy was staring, and Amber teared up. "Oh, damn."

"So, Annabelle got the money and bought me some scarves to fancy up my outfits, and that was the moment when Marko headed out and hijacked the babies because they knew they were needed."

Addy asked, "How much money is left?"

"I dunno. I don't have any accounts. There was no sense in installing a com or chip with me growing so rapidly. It would have been an irritating pain that I didn't really need at the time. I am stable now, thanks to Whee, but that is a new situation."

Addy sighed. "I am sorry. I got this so wrong." She scowled. "Who was the Citadel official who told you about the debt load?"

Mel frowned. "I didn't get her name. She was pale green and had a fin kind of thing on either side of her face. The hair was yellowy green and had a seaweed and mossy texture. She had a chipped front tooth and looked like she didn't have much use for Terrans."

Addy blinked. "Right. I think I know who Annabelle was talking to. We don't charge for rescue efforts if the personnel was on duty."

"She was on bodyguarding duty. She appears to be a heavy-hitter with an energy discharge." Mel shrugged. "Seems that she will have an easy time finding a new assignment or posting if she goes with the Guardians. She can fly, too."

Addy smiled. "I will leave a message on Rai. If she wants to come back, we would love her on Iratho."

"I think she will be on a journey of self-discovery for a while. I am not really able to be in contact with her. She needs to find out what is left of herself and what she can remake into something that works for her. I hope she becomes a florist." Mel smiled. "The world needs more flowers."

There was a low rumble coming from her shoulder, and Whee headbutted her father off them. Rumble flapped to regain his balance and return to Addy.

"I think the kids are rejecting curfew." She chuckled and petted the little ones, returning Pohloh to the other shoulder.

Addy picked Rumble up and blinked. "Your Yaluthu cursed at her. A lot."

"Oh, that's Marko's love language."

Pohloh was grumpy.

"They appear to be taking on heavy-grav characteristics," Amber stated.

"Well, some kind of Vendari adaptation as heavy-grav folks are usually shorter. Well, with a few exceptions." Mel shrugged. "I have just been able to start my education."

Amber frowned. "Really?"

"That kind of growth hurts like hell, makes it hard to concentrate. I was glad that Whee arrived after the worst of it."

We will work on your education. It was promised to you, and we will deliver.

She smiled slightly and murmured, "That would be interesting. I have never been able to get an education before."

Then, you shall have it and plenty of flowers.

Mel smiled.

Addy blinked. "You have a mate that talks in your head?"

"Um, I suppose."

"Do you want to know how to talk to him without speaking out loud?"

"Oh. Sure."

"You know how you talk to your... Whee?"

"Yes."

"Project that with words, and see if he can hear it."

"Hey, Ves. Can you hear this?"

I can always hear you, Mel. You don't need special effort.

"I don't want to look like a giant crazy person."

Ah, understandable. Right. Yes, I can understand you very well. This is very clear.

She looked to Addy. "How much did my lips move?"

Addy smiled. "Not at all."

"Yay. You taught me a thing."

Amber laughed.

They sat around, ate the snacks, and drank two more pots of tea.

When Marko returned, Mel sighed. "Well, ladies, thank you for the visit. I miss talking to people who don't have beaks."

Marko chortled, *"Fussy cow."*

She laughed and got to her feet. "It was nice properly meeting you, Adelheid, and lovely to meet you, Queen Amber."

Addy got up and extended her hand. "You don't shake hands?"

Mel smiled and extended two fingers. Addy looked at their hands and burst out laughing. "Okay, I get the point."

"Thank you. Amber, I will simply incline my head to you. I don't want any parts of you squished."

Amber smiled. "Thank you. I hope we can meet again soon."

Mel nodded, and they walked back to her shuttle. She held the littles toward Rumble, and there was a lot of head rubbing.

Mel looked at Addy. "When you see them again, they are going to be raptors. They are fluffing already."

Addy blinked. "Wow. That's fast."

She walked toward her ship, and Marko remained on her shoulder until she was standing on the ramp. "Thanks again for the very interesting visit. Have a great life." She waved at the ladies as they got to a safe distance.

She laughed and headed into the vessel, settling in and

smiling at the strange turn to a stressful day. She set the babies in with Marko, and Ves soon had them up and travelling.

The next stop was Vendar's territory and Occorin and his clone and Vendar himself.

CHAPTER EIGHT

"Are we there yet? Are we there yet? Are we there yet?" She thudded the basketball up and down the halls as she walked. Whee muttered a repeat of her tone as they moved through the ship.

Occorin's projection was in front of her, and she walked through him. "Stop doing that, Mel."

She grinned and kept walking. "Why? It's hilarious. Why did it take only a bit over a week to get to Possitt II, but we have been heading back home for three weeks?"

He projected further ahead. "Because planets move, and the station is moving. We have to make a course to have two moving objects intersect. We are nearly home. You will get to feel actual gravity under your feet."

She smiled and kept her slow walk with her basketball

down the hall until she reached the projection and dribbled slowly. "I will believe it when it happens."

Whee chirped confirmation. She was developing a jaded personality. She was making Mel proud.

Occorin looked at her and shook his head. "We are about to intercept the station."

"Like... when?"

The engines ceased, and the hum of the station pull started. "Now. Now would be when. So, yes, Melora. We are here."

"Where is here?"

"We are on the station, over Vendar."

"Oh, so all the things."

"Yes, and can you get yourself under control because we have a guest."

"A guest?" She looked down at her bodysuit and the sash that she now considered her daily uniform. The sash made her smile when she put it on.

"Yes. He will meet us on the station, and I am begging you to be on good behaviour."

"Why?"

"Because Vendar missed a deadline to offer you a home, and this representative can remove you from us."

She paused. "You are kidding."

"I am not kidding. He represents your avatar and can make that call."

"My speech patterns are rubbing off, so to speak. So, when do I meet with him?"

"We finish docking in two minutes, and he is right outside the door."

"Oh, are you sweating?"

"My body? Yes. Vendar? Yes. He has been very nervous to meet you, so he has been over-fussing on the home he made."

"Nervous?"

"There hasn't been a female Vendari in five thousand years."

"Oh, right. And that is how your folks got into trouble. All boys and really frisky."

"Correct."

"Which is why Vendar got excited when my genetics showed up."

"Also correct."

"So, has your body been altered to make girls?"

He smiled. "Correct again."

"Wow. I am really doing well today." There was a small thud under her feet. "So, I guess now is the time?"

"Please be on good behaviour."

She nodded and then whistled sharply. She started walking to the entry point of the ship when two thuds landed on her shoulder. Marko carried the very portly Pohloh and dropped her baby off before she settled with a tired sigh.

"Marko, she can run along the ground just fine. She's pretty fast."

Marko leaned over and said, *"Find a mirror, bitch."*

Mel laughed and walked to the door, waiting for the scan that would let her out.

The door swung open, and she walked out, looking for the visitor.

The man in the sleeveless bodysuit would have been terrifying if she had still been under six feet tall. As it was, she looked at the sleek black feathers that acted in place of his hair, and she grinned. "You are Alyla's dad. Imbolt-Zanican."

He looked at her with designs moving under his skin. "You know me?"

"I spent a lot of time with your daughter and saw some family photos."

He sighed. "I am sorry I was not there to manage your transformation. I could have made it faster and painless."

"I would not have said no to that, but I managed."

"What do you think of your mate?"

143

She paused and cocked her head. "May I be frank?"

"Please."

"While I have met projections, I have not met either Occorin or Vendar in person. That was supposed to happen today, I believe."

Imbolt scowled. "It was supposed to happen months ago. And Occorin and Vendar are in the same body."

She scowled. "That I do not appreciate."

Rushing feet approached them, and a male that was flushed or something that made his skin darker. "Imbolt-Zanican, forgive me. I was preparing a meal for her."

She nodded. "He does do that and medical assistance, and he made sure that I was still on the Rai Station when the Yaluthu came, and I am guessing he and they had a chat."

Occorin ducked his head. "It was short. They understood your need."

Imbolt looked at them. "You aren't enraged at him?"

"He's the only guy my size in the universe. I am not trying to pare down the dating pool. I can kick his ass later, after I stop wearing the restrictor suits."

Imbolt looked and narrowed his eyes. "What is it doing?"

"It keeps me from moving 'too big' on planets. The horseshit about me flying apart isn't really plausible for short situations, but this keeps me moving normally around smaller people so that I can manage it. I have some dresses without it and am looking forward to wearing them where I can twirl without anyone watching."

Imbolt scowled at Occorin. "Why wasn't her home ready?"

He mumbled, "When I saw her, it wasn't good enough for her, so I made a new home that is better with gardens and fountains and pools. Places for Marko and the Yaluthu. It has everything to act as a base between travels if she wants to travel."

Occorin looked at her hopefully.

Imbolt asked, "You have arranged food and clothing?"

"Yes. The bots have been planting and harvesting. Fresh fruit is there, and we are going to cultivate that fruit that she got on Veth to help hormonal shifts in case of pregnancy."

Imbolt smiled. "I heard about that. Now, what are your plans for a population?"

"Lottery system and an adaptation station next to our main station. It is already under construction."

Mel paused. "People want to live here?"

Occorin nodded. "But the qualifier was that no male would be in charge of any Vendari outpost. Our worlds are lush and peaceful. We are relatively safe from attack due to the gravity situation. If you are willing to adapt to heavy grav, it is a wonderful place to live."

"Whoa, so I am going to be in charge?"

"Yes, Melora, you will get the laws and the rules and the power to enforce them. Your education will begin now that the pain is gone."

Imbolt put his hand on his head. "You didn't tell her?"

Mel shrugged. "To be frank, I was in enough pain to cause me a lot of distraction. Learning anything wasn't plausible. To be fair, the Alliance didn't give me any information either, and I had a very long trip out here. It could have been added to my language and etiquette program at any time."

Imbolt blinked. "Oh, I—" His voice changed pitch and vibrated with energy. *"We apologize for the mishandling of your case. You are the first heavy-grav adaptation that has been deliberately created away from the world they are destined for, and your destiny changed frequently."*

Mel smiled. "No, it didn't. Vendar is just very good at mimicking other signal origins and body projections." She glanced at Occorin. "He wanted me transformed by inches, so to speak, so that my experience would not be all screaming."

OccorinA molten silver overtook Occorin's eyes. *"You understand more than we gave you credit for."*

146

"Well, frankly, it was Whee's addition that let me put things into perspective, and she helped me to hack into Ves's records so I could look up transformations into a heavy-worlder." She sighed. "They rarely survive. The pain is extreme and drives many to suicide." She grimaced. "The screaming was excessive."

Occorin flinched. "I didn't know what you were looking at. There was a firewall made of singing kittens that distracted me while the data was acquired and sealed off, and the trail was erased."

Mel shrugged. "Well, I have been on the station and ship for months. I picked up a few things."

Imbolt frowned. "Where did you get the kitten images?"

Mel grinned. "Alyla. She felt like hell over my situation and did whatever it took to help."

Occorin-Vendar looked at her. *"Interesting. Are you willing to see your home at long last?"*

"Well, I just saw my mate, so why not the house."

Imbolt paused. "This is your first time seeing him?"

"In person? Yes. He has been a projection on the ship for this whole time but only made himself visible in the last month or so."

"So, you have not consummated your connection?"

She chuckled. "I haven't even shaken his hand."

Imbolt asked softly, "You aren't feeling uncontrollably aroused?"

"Um, no. He's pretty colours and all, but I am more aroused by a good dessert lately." She shrugged.

He exhaled and looked at Vendar's avatar. "You have kept your word but not your timing. Earn her touch, and let me know if you need anything. When you are ready, the candidates will come."

"Candidates?"

Occorin smiled. "We need a population, and since there are only a few who could be citizens, we have to take those who want the heavy-grav adaptation and run a medical centre to create it."

"Oh. Will it hurt them?"

"We will use sedation and tanks. They are not being changed to our height. That was the cause of most of your discomfort."

"Got it."

Imbolt scowled. "We should adjourn to the surface so I can make sure it is suitable, Melora."

"Okay. Sure." She looked to Occorin. "Are we good to head down?"

He nodded. "If you will come with me?" He held out his hand, and she blinked.

She slowly extended her hand to him, and his fingers closed around hers. He smiled at her shyly, and she smiled in return. "I hope you like feathers. Whee has started moulting, and she needs a place to nest."

He smiled. "I hope you both find it suitable for making yourselves comfortable."

She nodded. "Back to the shuttle?"

"No. We are using a drop-ship. Zanican can get himself up and down and back to his ship."

Mel looked at the other avatar, and he grinned and nodded.

She nodded. "Right. So, I finally get to see where I am going to be living."

Occorin kissed her knuckles, and she smiled slightly. With her buddies on her shoulders, she was walked to the drop shuttle, strapped into the chair, and each of her little ones had their own safety seats. Occorin sat at the controls, and the ship they were in lifted off and cruised down a long hall until they were near the field that kept the atmosphere in. They punched through, and then she saw Vendar for the first time.

"Oh, it's beautiful. Wait. It looks like us."

Occorin laughed. "It does. That was on purpose."

She blinked and saw a mountain sculpted in the profile of her face. "Wow. This is like a messed-up theme park."

"He wanted to make sure that you knew he wanted you here. The execution has been rough, but the intent is to your benefit."

The ship eased into the atmosphere and glided toward a structure made of stepped-down gardens leading to a fairy castle. A waterfall came out of the upper level and cascaded down to fill a pool that fed the gardens.

"Oh, wow."

Occorin exhaled slowly. "He is very glad you like it. Your past has been so hostile that he wanted to make sure you felt serene here. This is a place for new starts, so he wanted it to be beautiful."

He flew around the castle and settled on a gravel pad. "Your clothing was wrapped up and packed on board."

"Oh. Cool," she murmured, but her eyes took in a light spectrum that she didn't even know she could see. There were colours that she didn't have names for, and she wanted to learn them.

Occorin undid his latches, and as she did the same, he opened the safety pods and helped her menagerie out.

"How are you feeling?"

She shrugged. "The same as on the station."

She got up and loaded her crew onto her shoulders.

Occorin took her hand and led her out onto her new world.

They went through the castle, and her eyes took in all the details. Marko was flying, and Whee was in the bedroom making a nest out of Mel's favourite sash.

When they joined Imbolt in the kitchen, he was sitting and talking on his com to his daughter. He glanced up. "And here they are."

Mel called out, "Hi, Alyla."

The hologram turned to see her. "*Mel. Oh, gosh. You look amazing. Marko, you are stunning.*"

"Thank you, Alyla."

"*Pretty birdie!*"

Alyla paused. "*Did Marko just speak without cursing?*"

Mel smiled. "She feels it's a bad influence on the young ones."

"*Wow.*"

"Yeah. How have you been keeping?"

"*Well, we have a number of other Resets lined up for when Dad gets home.*"

"You are taking good care of them?"

"No one is in a hurry. One is a half-Lrrko, and they are shocked that she showed up."

Imbolt blinked. "I thought that all of them had been found."

"Yes, and no. One of them had their ovaries extracted, and based on the existence of this woman, she was born shortly after that event. Someone used the harvested eggs."

Mel asked, "How is that a reset?"

"Lrrko have different attributes. She needs to let her dominant genes come to the surface. In her case, it is a makeover." Alyla shrugged. *"They are going to send a representative for her, but things are a little complicated."*

"Why?"

"She doesn't like the way he looks. Her instinct is to make him prettier when he arrives, and he isn't going for it."

"Prettier, how?"

"She's a tattoo artist."

"Oh. Wow. Does she do heavy-grav skin?"

"I can ask. She might need a pressure suit."

Occorin asked, "You would mark your skin?"

"Yes. I always wanted some tattoos. I think that designing something for the position I suddenly find myself in would be cool."

Imbolt asked, "Like what?"

"A thick band of gold across my shoulders and wrapping around to keep the band even. And then, if I have kids, add one after each one."

Occorin swallowed. "You are willing to have children with me?"

"Well, pace yourself. I still haven't done more than touch your hand. Not even a hug."

He nodded. "I was hoping we would be alone for that or, at least, as alone as it was possible to be."

Imbolt asked, "Melora, are you satisfied with this situation?"

"I am satisfied that this is a good start. I am here to start over again, not just wallow." She smiled. "As Ves, he was there for everything I needed, and anything he couldn't figure out himself, he asked other Terrans. He attempted to provide me with a social network. The Yaluthu were brought on board by him for assistance and pacification. If he is from a species where the men ask for help, I will gladly sign up to start the next generation."

Imbolt smiled. "I wasn't aware of those other actions, and that is easing my worry a bit."

Mel smiled. "Good. It sounds like your daughter needs you."

He frowned. "I am going to return in six months, and you had better be settled and happy."

She laughed. "I will probably be settled, but happy is up to me. I am getting there. Whee is helping a lot."

Imbolt said, "May I give you a hug?"

"Sure, but don't make it weird."

He laughed, disconnected the call to his daughter, and then came around to hug her. He separated and said, "The dysmorphia is usually dealt with in the tubes with audio counselling."

"Well, I am good with me now anyway. It took a bit, but I think I am nearly there."

"Minerva will be pleased. She's been worried."

"Her and me both. Now, scoot, Imbolt-Zanican. I look forward to your return in six months."

He smiled. "I need to talk to Occorin-Vendar first, but thank you for your dismissal."

She grinned. "I am going to be out in the gardens if anyone is curious."

She left the avatars alone and carried her buddies outside.

Looking around, she used her com and sent a call. "Hey,

Minerva. How are you doing?"

"Melora? Oh, my. How are you doing? How are you settling in?"

"I just arrived at Vendar today. It looks nice. He put a lot of effort into making something I would like."

"Wait. You just got there today? Imbolt said you were on your way months ago."

"There were detours, and as Vendar has lost his entire population once, he wanted to make sure that I would be content with limited interaction with others. He is trying to prove that this time he will be different."

Minerva smiled. *"That is progress. Hey, you have a com!"*

"Yeah. I am as tall as I am getting, and nine feet is enough for anybody. A Yaluthu found me and has stopped the panic in my brain. Whee is almost about to have her little ones. The first high-grav Yaluthu."

Minerva sighed. *"Crossing my fingers that there is only one."*

"And Marko's Yaluthu is going to have some as well."

Minerva gasped. *"Marko has her own Yaluthu?"*

"Yes. Its name is Pohloh."

"Marko-polo... oy." Minerva smacked her forehead.

"I get my fun where I can. Speaking of, Imbolt is inside chatting with Occorin."

"*You mean, Zanican is talking with Vendar. If your sector is lighting up again, there will be a lot of heavy grav and just folks who want the quiet life coming in. So much vetting of the files.*"

"Well, I guess it will be fun to learn if I get to participate."

Minerva smiled. "*You will be. Congrats on getting a com.*"

"You said that."

"*Yeah, but that is high speed. You have consul privileges.*"

"Neat."

"*You don't know what that means.*" Minerva smiled.

"Nope. But I finally have time to start learning, and Whee is calming me enough that I can remember important stuff." She smiled. "I can breathe. I am not in pain anymore. I know that I will make it through the night and Marko is safe. Anything else is just a bonus."

"*What about Occorin?*"

"He's nice. He's thoughtful and careful, sometimes too careful. At this point, I just want to jump him and strip him just to find how everything works at this scale."

Minerva coughed and flicked her fingers.

"How long have they been behind me?"

"*Two minutes. Nothing more.*"

She turned, and Occorin looked slightly embarrassed, but Imbolt was grinning wide.

She muttered, "Gotta go, bye." She stopped the call and looked at the two avatars. "How much did you hear?"

Occorin smiled slightly. "There is a perfectly good bed in your room if you want to check the specs of a Vendaran."

Imbolt chuckled. "On that note, I am content that things are progressing in a positive manner, and the residence cannot be faulted. I will see you in five months, Melora."

"See you. Hug Alyla for me."

"I will. Vendar, glad that you are back in the universe again." Imbolt's eyes glowed, and he simply hovered and then flew away from the surface.

"Oh, right. Avatar." She watched him fly off and then looked at Occorin-Vendar. "Fine. Down to basics, what actually happened to your people?"

Vendar's eyes widened, but he sighed. "I made them powerful and arrogant and irresistible. I occupied myself with minimizing natural disasters and pretended the people just loved them, not that they were hurting their populations. So, a council of avatars was convened, and I had to destroy my people. I didn't kill them; I isolated them and sterilized them. They died out in less than a century, and my worlds went quiet. That was two thousand years ago, by your reckoning. I have been silent ever since, just maintaining my worlds. When Zanican mentioned the project, I put my genetic requirements out there. You appeared, and it was a scramble to get my one remaining body out of cold storage and functioning, so I used a cybernetic form to get the house ready and rejoined Occorin when we were ready for you."

She blinked. "So, you had to destroy the people you had designed to live on your worlds because they were unstable and bratty, and yes, I have an idea of what they got up to because people fall all over themselves to do whatever I need, and some needs are louder than others."

Occorin looked at her cautiously. "You are referring to sex?"

"I am not referring to board games. Why do you think I play so much basketball? I need to equalize the blood flow." She looked at him. "How do we stop the next generations from becoming the same kind of self-entitled assholes?"

"The next generations will have something that my first gen didn't have. A mother. I have no doubt that you will pull in any misbehaviour. We will also have high-grav Yaluthu for those who have emotional issues now. That is a lovely piece of chance, but I am holding onto anything that will offer a calm future."

She smiled. "I like the uncertainty. I can live with that. You can adapt to uncertainty."

Occorin smiled. "You are willing to try with me?"

"I am willing to adapt with you."

He grinned and eased her toward him, making eye contact with the Yaluthu and Marko. He angled his head and kissed her.

Her body reacted like she thought it would. She had been remade for him and that was what she was feeling. She sighed as the kiss started and kept going.

She saw a flash of light in the sky, broke the kiss, and shouted, "Stop peeping, Imbolt!"

There was a thread of laughter in the air as they returned to their first kiss on their first world on their first day together.

* * * *

Six months later.

Mel watched the shuttle slowly descend to the spaceport, which she just considered the back-backyard. Vendar spoke softly in her thoughts. *Are you ready to greet the new arrivals, Melora?*

"Yup. I am going." She used a bit of the energy that he had

provided her with and flew slowly to the shuttle area as it settled.

She landed near the ramp, and Marko and Whee were with her. Pohloh was at home nesting. It had finally gotten to the point where it wanted to spawn.

Occorin was in the city getting the residences ready for the new citizens.

As she thought of him, he landed next to her and kissed her quickly. "Did I miss them?"

"The new high-grav citizens? Nope."

He kept his arm on her back, and they stood together as they watched the first members of their carefully chosen population. Different ages and different species, they all wanted to live quietly on a high-gravity world, and Vendar fit the bill.

They stood as the cargo ramp descended with the new colonists slowly lining up and walking down toward the hard surface of the landing area.

Mel shifted from foot to foot as she waited for a familiar face, and when she saw her, she walked forward. "Annabelle!"

Annabelle ran toward her and thudded into her with a solid thud. "Mel! You are looking great."

"Thanks. So, where is he?"

Annabelle looked behind her and smiled as the Rai walked down the ramp behind them. "Hai-sko, this is my friend Melora of Terra, bride of Vendar, companion to Yaluthu, and queen of the Vendari."

Hai-sko was dressed in a battlesuit covered by an open kimono in the manner of Rai Guardians. Annabelle was dressed in the kimono of a lady of Rai.

"You look lovely, Annabelle."

"Thank you. I couldn't believe it when I made up my mind to come here, and Hai-sko was in the same high-grav prep class."

Hai-sko came up to them and stood behind Annabelle.

"You don't mind the one-way trip?"

Annabelle smiled. "I need stability. I need a place just to be me. This entire world is starting over, and that energy is a powerful draw."

Hai-sko said, "My family is gone, and a new start on a new world appealed to me. If you don't mind our effect on local fashions, we will be happy to make a home here."

Annabelle smiled. "I got into silk painting. He's from a family of kimono makers. I see you have gone casual."

Mel knew that her skirt and light top were fluttering in the breeze, matching what Occorin was wearing. They looked like they were on a Caribbean vacation in silky pyjamas.

She nodded. "We are still in search of a traditional costume."

Hai-sko asked, "What are the wedding rituals here?"

Mel paused. She couldn't say that a post-coital high-five had sealed the deal. "Let's start a council of new arrivals, and we can set up rituals, holidays, and that sort of thing."

Occorin smiled. "Hello again, Annabelle. You are looking much better now."

"Ves?"

"Occorin-Vendar." Mel smiled. "Ves when we are on the station."

Annabelle smiled. "Taller than I thought."

He smiled and inclined his head.

Mel looked to Whee. "Oh, this is Whee. She's my buddy and a Yaluthu. She has had one fluffle. Her sibling is Marko's Yaluthu, and she is currently having her fluffles. Its name is Pohloh."

Annabelle caught it immediately. "Oh, my god." She giggled.

Hai-Sko asked, "What is the amusement?"

"I will explain it later, but it is a child's game." Annabelle grinned. "So, where are we staying?"

The bots were organizing their shipmates and getting the cargo.

Mel realized she was the hostess. She walked over and said, "Good day to you all. I am Melora of Terra, now of Vendar. I am half of the Avatar of Vendar; the other half is Occorin. I would like to welcome you here and thank you for volunteering to start out all new on a new world. We are all finding our way here, so if there is something you feel is missing from your life here, mention it. If it is a mate, we have twenty thousand applications for new citizens right now. Just file your requests and specifics, and we will filter those available persons and move them to the front of the list."

She breathed in. "And if you are looking for multiples, do keep in mind that not everyone feels that way. There will be no force, drugging, coercion, manipulation, blackmailing, or anything else of other members of the population. Punishable by being turned into paste and being used as fertilizer. All unions have to be registered for consent. Even temporary ones."

The colonists looked at each other. One woman asked, "Why?"

"Because the previous Vendar used and abused the people

on their worlds, at will. They took without asking, so this time, we are putting that in the regulations. First, you ask, and when the answer is yes, you are free to go and do whatever in as large a group as you can manage." Mel smiled.

Occorin chuckled. "Now, let's walk to the city centre, and you will be assigned your quarters until things are settled and you choose your occupations and locations."

He put his hand on her back, and they walked into the enormous city with the bots carrying everything ahead of them. The consent registrations were every three blocks, so there was no way that it wouldn't be covered for the next population. It was a stupid thing to focus on, but it had caused the extinction of the species. This was a step that she was willing to take. If they were able to eradicate the early issues, more would crop up, but Mel had to live a life, and no one was going to mess with her second chance.

Mel breathed in deeply and looked at Marko with a smile. She looked at Occorin and felt Vendar behind her eyes. It looked like it was second chances all around, and they were bringing the new volunteers into their reset.

Author's Note

So, Mel's story was... different. She really needed to go through some things to get to the starting gate... at the end of the book. It's odd, but you have read stranger.

Thanks for reading,

Viola Grace

ABOUT THE AUTHOR

Viola Grace is a Canadian author who immerses herself in Fantasy, Paranormal, Sci-Fi, and graphic novels (that's new). Writing for a few decades, she has spanned short stories, novellas, novels, and the occasional collaboration with the result being an astonishingly large backlist.

Focusing her work on humour, lightness of spirit, and now and then a heat level to scorch the pages, she leaves the dark and depressing to others. Happily ever afters are guaranteed.

The crafts she has accrued over her lifetime regularly work their way into her books with a variety of results for the characters.

When she's at home, she is usually hiding indoors with felines of various sizes. The bees come in one size, and their speed is usually fast. When she is outdoors, she takes pictures of the stunning skies above her home and the wildness of nature that surrounds her, imagining fantastical worlds hiding in everything around her.